The Cowboy and
the Thief

Published by Phaze Books
Also by Mychael Black & Shayne Carmichael

The Power of Two (eBook)
Kitten (print collection)
Onyx
Dominion (eBook)
*The Adventures of Captain Chase Sykes
and Navigator Duncan Sampson*
Dark Needs (print collection)
The Duke's Husband
Through the Dark
When I Dream of You

By Shayne only

Tombstone Ranch
Snap Decision
The Guardian

Cincinnati, Ohio

www.Phaze.com

The Cowboy and the Thief

a short novel of homoerotic romance by

MYCHAEL BLACK
SHAYNE CARMICHAEL

Cincinnati, Ohio

A Phaze Production
Phaze Books
6470A Glenway Avenue, #109
Cincinnati, OH 45211-5222
Phaze is an imprint of Mundania Press, LLC.

To order additional copies of this book, contact:
books@phaze.com
www.Phaze.com

Cover art © 2008 Debi Lewis
Edited by Kathryn Lively

Trade Paperback ISBN-13: 978-1-60659-028-7

First Print Edition – August, 2008
Printed in the United States of America

10 9 8 7 6 5 4 3 2 1

PART ONE

Jamie grunted and kept his teeth tight on the pencil as he moved carefully across the scaffolding, measuring the width of the window. This definitely had to be the biggest job he'd ever gotten, and certainly the most lucrative. Eric DeSalvo was one of the most well-known—and the richest—private collector of art and 'treasures' in New Brunswick, and he'd paid Jamie a substantial figure to work for him.

Five feet wide. Damn. Jamie shook his head and leaned down carefully, fumbling blindly for the small pad where he kept his notes. Soon as he had it, and he jotted down the dimensions for one of the stained glass windows he had to make: five feet wide by six feet tall. Good Lord Almighty. There were nine more windows Eric wanted as well.

Setting his Stetson back a bit, a lock of black hair fell forward, almost covering his right eye as he watched the few people milling about—five feet below.

As a man entered the house, he looked around. The butler approached him and bowed his head to him.

"Is Eric anywhere nearby, Smith?"

"Mr. DeSalvo is in conference right now, but he wants you to wait for him, Mr. Williams."

"No problem, I guess." Shrugging, the man turned away from the butler and moved to the one of the chairs against the wall.

Jamie turned and watched as the new arrival sat down. *Damn fine.* Jamie wondered what such a young man would be doing at Eric DeSalvo's private estate. Turning slowly so as not to shake the scaffolding too much, Jamie finally managed to climb down, almost jumping to his feet right in front of... *Oh. Very pretty.*

"Sorry if I startled you," he said. Tucking the tape measure into his shirt pocket, he tipped his hat at the man.

The young man jumped slightly, surprised to see Jamie.

"Nah, it's okay." After eyeing the scaffolding, his gaze turned back to the cowboy. "Out of curiosity, what's going on? Or is it a top secret project?"

Looking up, Jamie chuckled. "Name's Jamie Holland. Mr. DeSalvo commissioned me to do several windows — stained glass." He took in the young man's features, trying not to look like he was doing it. Lord, the man was sweet lookin'. Eyes the color of the finest sherry, sweet lips just beggin' for a kiss. *Oh yeah, he looks fine. Mighty fine.*

"Seems like we're both here on business. I'm Adrian Williams." As he stood up, he held out his hand, offering it to Jamie. "Pleasure to meet you."

Jamie resisted the temptation to lick his lips. Or, better yet, lick Adrian's lips. Lord, what he could imagine. He shook his head quickly as he took Adrian's hand. "Pleasure's mine," he said, tipping his hat again. "So what're you here for? Or is *that* secret?" He gave Adrian a quick wink, his voice a smooth Texas drawl.

"I find things Eric wants and get them for him." A casual shrug accompanied the words, and after a moment he let go of Jamie's hand.

A loud voice reverberated from one of the halls. "Damn pink elephants. Get the hell out of my house."

Rolling his eyes, Adrian lowered his voice, "I'm guessing Uncle Albert had a bit too much brandy again."

Jamie blinked. "Uncle—Albert? Lord, Lord. What have I left Texas for?"

Before Adrian could say another, a workman suddenly careened around the corner, seeming to flee from something. The sound of shouted curses added to the confusion before an old man rounded the corner, madly waving a cane as he chased the workman.

Adrian grabbed Jamie's arm and pulled him back closer to the wall. "You'll want to get out of the way. That damn cane hurts."

Jamie tried to focus on the bizarre fiasco playing out in front of them, and not on the hand on his arm. He certainly wasn't paying attention to the way Adrian moved—sleek like a cat, graceful and easy. He ignored the way every stitch of clothing seemed to slide across that slender, muscular frame.

Fuck. Fuck, fuck, fuck.

Licking his lips, he forced himself to absolutely not look at Adrian's mouth. "Dare I even ask what's going on?"

Pointing in the general direction of the wildly raving Albert, Adrian said as low as could, "That's Eric's Uncle Albert. Rather senile and even more so when he sneaks into Eric's brandy. For some reason, he thinks the poor guy is a pink elephant. Pink elephants are the bane of Uncle Albert's brandy habits."

The room became quiet again when the workman fled outside and the old man followed

8

him.

"Uh-huh." Jamie just nodded, a bit too stunned to move. "Well, that was certainly worth a beer or ten." He flipped through his notepad briefly, color prints of previous jobs taped to some of the pages.

Adrian didn't seem at all phased by what had just happened. Glancing down at the pad, he looked over what he could see. Before Jamie could turn it, he held out his hand to the page. "Damn, that's some nice work."

"Huh? Oh!" Jamie laughed. "Thanks. These are nothin' compared to my portfolio." He gave a long, low whistle. "You should see some of those."

"Probably cost an arm and leg, too." Withdrawing the hand, it fell back to Adrian's side.

Jamie shrugged. "Depends, really. I've done a variety of pieces, for a variety of prices. Just depends on what the customer wants." He looked over his notes, then slipped the notepad into the front pocket of his shirt. He opened his mouth to say something more, but DeSalvo's butler appeared at the top of the stairs.

"Mr. Williams, Mr. DeSalvo will see you now."

"Damn," Jamie muttered under breath.

When Adrian stepped forward, a loud crash came from upstairs near the second floor landing. A second later, a large red parrot flew down the stairs, chased by a small red-headed boy.

"I believe Alto and Jeremy have escaped their cages yet again, Smith."

With a harried look, the poor butler chased down the stairs after the two as he yelled, "Nanny Jenkins!"

Turning to look at Jamie, he murmured, "You get used to it around here."

With a bit of a smile and a wink, Adrian turned on his heel to head towards Eric's office.

* * * *

A cool breeze blowing in through the open door of the studio, a cold beer, and Brooks and Dunn on the little radio. Yeah. Jamie was doing fine, mighty fine. Three orders in the last week, plus DeSalvo's work—good pieces, good work, good pay. He couldn't quite ask for more, except maybe a quick dip in the pool at the apartments. Damn, it was hot. Not quite as hot as Texas, but still damned hot. Then there was the thought of that sweet piece of work—Adrian Williams. Oh, yeah. Now that's a hot Jamie would gladly take.

It had taken him a few days to work out the details for the first window DeSalvo wanted. The design would be an intricate portrait in glass of Michael and Lucifer. He'd drawn a couple of preliminary sketches, and had just begun working the dimensions for the glass.

Hearing the jingle of the bells on the front door, Jamie emerged from the back, wiping hands on his faded jeans. "Can I help...? Oh. Hi there." A slow smile spread across his lips as he neared Adrian and the woman beside him. "Fancy meeting you again."

"Damn, Lucy, must you tell complete strangers what idiots they are?" Giving her a harassed look, Adrian eyed her severely.

"But, Adrian, he was a total jerk. And his girlfriend did try to come onto me." Rolling her eyes, she ignored Adrian as she looked around at the store.

Her gaze riveted on the sparkling glass in a bowl on one of the tables. "Oh—those are so pretty."

It took Adrian a moment to notice Jamie was in the room. Blinking rapidly, it was another second before Adrian held out his hand to Jamie. "Oh, hey. Now this is a surprise."

A rather bemused grin accompanied the gesture. "Hi there, yourself." He tipped his hat at the young woman named Lucy. "Howdy, ma'am. Can I help you two? Lookin' for anything in particular? Custom work?"

When Lucy noticed Jamie, she walked right up to him. "A pretty cowboy. I like him. Baxter likes him too, don't you, Baxter?"

When she finished speaking, she reached for Jamie and gave him a hug. "My rabbit thinks you're pretty, too. I'm Lucy in the Sky with Diamonds. Who are you?"

Adrian just stepped back, trying to signal Jamie silently with his eyes to tolerate the young woman and humor her.

Jamie's eyes went wide, but he returned the hug. "Nice namesake," he laughed. "It's a pleasure. I'm Jamie Holland, owner of Texas Glass and the artist of all the pieces you see here."

With a slight tilt of her head, she studied Jamie with a very serious look. Reaching up with her hand, she lightly patted him on the cheek. "You'll do. You'll do very nicely. And you're a very sweet man, too, Jamie."

Pulling away from him, Lucy moved towards a tray filled with glass nuggets and began to play with them.

"I'll...do?" Jamie shot Adrian a quizzical look, one dark eyebrow lifting.

Adrian gave him a rueful look as he moved closer to Jamie. Lowering his voice, he said, "Sorry, we ducked in here to avoid some people Lucy pissed off. She's..." Adrian paused, trying to come up with a word but failed. "She's Lucy. It's hard telling what she's talking about. It's probably Baxter talking to her again."

"Baxter?" Jamie asked, looking again at Lucy, watching her play with the glass pieces in the bowl. "She's...unique. I'll give you that. So, you two...? Together?"

"Baxter is the rabbit on her shirt." Blinking owlishly at Jamie for the suggestion of him and Lucy together, he said, "Nah, she's my cousin. I keep an eye out for her."

"Oh." Jamie glanced over at Adrian, wondering if he should just ask the kid outright how old he was and if he was game. But he simply couldn't get his mouth to form the damned words. Instead, he just laughed and moved over to the counter, bending over it to turn off the radio.

Lucy seemed quite content playing with the pretty pieces of rounded glass. Occasionally she'd hold one up and peer through it intently before carefully laying it back down.

Adrian watched Jamie's movement as he bent over. "Nice ass there."

Jamie just froze where he was. "Well. That certainly answers one of my questions," he said with a chuckle. He switched off the radio and turned, jumping up onto the counter. Leaning back, he braced himself on his hands. "Now for the other. How old are you anyway?"

Adrian answered him quickly and asked his own question as well. "Twenty-four. Why? Does it matter?"

"It could," Jamie murmured with a nod, his tongue slowly wetting his lips. "You play?"

"With you?" Never one to mince words, Adrian smiled. "It's a damn good chance, though it depends on what you mean by play."

Jamie's smile was slow and easy, his thighs parting just as smooth. The faded denim of his jeans revealed a not-so-small bulge. "Depends on what you like," he said, voice going low, the Texas drawl smooth and deep.

Stepping closer to Jamie, he kept his voice at a level to remain unheard by his cousin. "Oh, I like the feel of fucking tight asses."

His gaze dropped to the crotch of Jamie's pants. "And I'm seeing you like the idea."

"All cowboys like to ride," Jamie said, the words almost a purr. "Especially this one. A hard, long ride…"

Stopping just short of Jamie, Adrian asked, "And how soon does this cowboy want to be ridden?"

From his expression, it'd be easy to tell Adrian thought his day had just gotten a hell of a lot better.

Jamie licked his lips, his gaze sliding slowly over Adrian's body. "I close shop in about an hour." He slid off the counter, the move bringing him within inches of Adrian. Focusing on Adrian's mouth, Jamie smiled. "Wanna ride you. Think you can do that? Let an old cowboy ride?"

Staring back at him, Adrian leaned slightly towards Jamie as he brought up his hand. The tip of one finger trailed lightly beneath the line of the cowboy's jaw. "That's just long enough to get my cousin home. Then come back and give you the ride you want."

Shooting a quick glance at Lucy proved the young girl was thoroughly entranced by the array of small pieces she'd laid out. Jamie caught Adrian's hand and pulled that finger into his mouth, rolling his tongue around it, a soft purr slipping free as he held Adrian's gaze. "One hour," he whispered.

Adrian's eyes widened slightly as he watched him, the tightening in his jeans an obvious reaction. "Oh, yeah, I'll be back, Jamie. I'll be back."

His fingers traced slowly over Jamie's lower lip before he dropped his hand. Turning away, he headed towards his cousin and took her arm. "Come on, Lucy, it's time to get home."

He led her, even as she protested, towards the door.

Jamie watched them leave, licking his lips. "I'll definitely be here, pretty boy."

* * * *

It was more like forty minutes before Adrian returned. Quietly he entered the shop, looking around for Jamie.

"In the back, Adrian," Jamie called. He was bent over his worktable, scoring a sheet of cobalt blue glass along an intricate pattern. "Come on back."

Hearing Jamie's voice, he headed towards the back. "Caught you while you were busy, didn't I?"

"Mm…" Jamie hummed along with the music

14

from the radio. "Nonsense." He set the glass cutter to the side and turned. "For a taste of that, I'll drop everything I'm doin'."

When he dropped the cutter, Adrian moved in on him. "Then why don't you close up shop early, Jamie? I'm dying to try out that mouth of yours."

Adrian wasn't one to beat around the bush when he wanted something.

Jamie gave him a quick wink and stepped around him. With a turn of the lock and a flip of the 'open' sign to 'closed,' Jamie showed himself to be more than ready for a bit of fun. He went back to where Adrian waited in the back room, then plastered himself square against the man, tongue sliding across Adrian's lips, slow and easy.

"Wanna taste," he purred. "Want you to fuck my mouth with that sweet prick."

The small flick of his tongue answered Jamie as Adrian reached for his hand. Drawing it down, he pressed it against the front of his pants. "I think you can see just how eager I am to do that."

Releasing Jamie's hand, his own moved up to unfasten his pants and unzip them before he rubbed the back of it over Jamie's jeans. Adrian felt completely at ease with a temporary sexual situation, and he was as hard as a rock.

Eyes locked onto Adrian's, Jamie slid his hand down into Adrian's pants, fingertips stroking the tip of Adrian's cock, spreading the sticky pre-come over it. Then he brought his fingers to his mouth, licking them clean.

"Taste good," he whispered, eyes smoldering. "Sweet. I fucking hate the taste of Latex, though.

Warn me before you shoot."

Watching him, Adrian's tongue wet his lips in an unconscious gesture. "I'm clean, but I'm not one to take chances since I want to stay that way. I did come prepared."

A light tug from Adrian's hands within the strands of Jamie's hair encouraged him to the right position.

Jamie went down easy, hands tugging Adrian's pants and underwear down as he went. Adrian's cock bobbed before him, bumping Jamie's lips. "Mm," he hummed softly, taking the shaft in one hand as he slid his lips along the length, "so fucking hot. Like molten silk." His eyes rolled up to watch Adrian as he opened his mouth to give the head a sucking kiss.

An easy smile tugged at Adrian's lips as his gaze followed Jamie going down on his knees. "Fucking hot view."

The light suction made Adrian's hips nudge slightly forward in anticipation of feeling Jamie's entire mouth. His fingers gently ran through Jamie's hair before tightening slightly in it.

"C'mon, pretty boy. Fuck my mouth like you mean it." With that, Jamie opened up, lips sliding down over Adrian's cock until his nose touched the dark brown curls around the base. He hummed low, the vibrations working straight through the flesh in his mouth. As one hand curled to Adrian's hip, the other cupped his balls, tugging them and rolling them gently.

"Fucking shit." Muttering the words, his eyes widened slightly with the vibration of sensation. It took little for Adrian to follow Jamie's suggestion.

Adrian's fingers held tightly to his hair as his hips moved. Several quick movements repeatedly slid the length deep into Jamie's mouth.

Jamie moaned and hummed, head moving back and forth, just letting Adrian fuck his mouth. He stroked his tongue along the underside, flicking it along the ridge just beneath the head before swallowing it whole once more. He kneaded Adrian's balls, rolling the hot sac in his palm as he pressed on the soft skin just behind them.

The surge rolling through Adrian made him groan though his eyes remained opened, watching Jamie. Several long moments of thrusting into Jamie's hot, willing mouth had his body visibly trembling. His other hand moved to circle his fingers around the base of his own cock as he muttered in a half groan. "Gonna come, Jamie. Fuck, I'm gonna come."

With the words, he pulled out of Jamie's mouth right before he did. His fingers stroked over himself as his body shuddered with the spill of thick, white liquid.

Biting at his bottom lip, Jamie watched, eyes hungry and hot. "Sweet. God, I wanna taste," he groaned, fingers working his jeans open as quickly as possible. When his cock sprang free, he started stroking, thumb rubbing the tip as he drank in the sight of Adrian slumped against the wall, cock hanging limp in his hands. "Shit. Adrian…"

Adrian leaned against the wall, trying to catch his breath as he watched Jamie jerk himself off. A lazy smile curled his lips as he grabbed for one of the work towels on Jamie's table and wiped his hand off.

Removing his own pants the rest of the way,

both Adrian's shirt and the pants ended up somewhere on the table. Without a word, Adrian pulled Jamie to his feet, and his hand took over, expertly running over the cowboy's cock in smooth strokes.

"Sweet Jesus," Jamie groaned. "Gonna come..." Eyes rolling back, he let out a long, throaty moan as he came, cock pumping in Adrian's fist. He shuddered and slumped against Adrian, breath coming hard. "Damn."

As Adrian held to him, one hand slipped around to caress the firm line of his ass. "I'm hoping it won't be the only time you'll be coming. Or me either."

Now the edge was off both of them, they would have a little more leisure time to enjoy each other. Adrian's lips sought Jamie's in a slow, melting kiss. The lazy stroke of his tongue seeking its own taste of the cowboy.

"Mm..." Jamie's arms draped around Adrian's neck, his tongue warring lazily with Adrian's. "S'good," he whispered on Adrian's lips. "Feels good..." His words trailed off as he dove back into the kiss, tongue sliding into Adrian's mouth to lick and taste. He stroked his hand over Adrian's hair, tilting Adrian's head just enough to add a bit of slow-burning heat to the kiss.

A low murmur could have been his own agreement with Jamie's words. Adrian remained busy, exploring Jamie's mouth. The fire seemed to be easily ignited between them. His fingers kneaded gently over Jamie's ass as he wiped off his hand on the nearby towel. Closing the space between their bodies, he leaned against Jamie.

"Yeah," Jamie purred, leaning back against the wall, tugging Adrian close. He rocked between Adrian's body and his hand, pushing back before grinding forward, his cock slowly waking. "Gonna give this ol' cowboy a run for his money? Gonna let 'im ride that sweet young prick?" The words brushed over Adrian's lips, the drawl smooth and thick.

Sliding his hand between them, Adrian caught both of their cocks and stroked over them, pressing them tightly together. "I'd be more than happy to oblige you."

Already aroused again, Adrian leaned slightly over, feeling for his pants and finally found the back pocket. Tugging on a condom, he pulled it out. "I told you, I did come prepared."

Jamie licked his lips and took the package from Adrian's hand. With a quick wink, he ripped it open and had Adrian sheathed within seconds. Then he turned and braced himself, palms flat against the wall. Bending at the waist a bit, he pushed his ass back, spreading his thighs, balls and cock swaying slightly beneath.

"C'mon," he urged, looking at Adrian over his shoulder. "Ride me hard and deep."

His gaze dropped to Jamie's ass, tight and muscular. One finger slid slowly downward over the crack of his ass before stilling to stroke over the tight ring of muscle. If Jamie wanted it hard and deep, that would be exactly what he'd get.

As Adrian reached around for Jamie's cock, he entered him, the slick condom providing the necessary lubrication. After a determined push of his hips, he felt himself slip deeper past the initial tight resistance. Sensation tugged at Adrian's brain and body, and at this point, he was definitely thinking only with his cock.

"Oh. Fuck, yes." Jamie's head dropped forward, all feeling directed to his ass and his cock. The stretch was fucking exquisite, especially after so long without anything there. Groaning, he rocked back, driving Adrian's cock deeper inside him. "Oh, God. Yeah, Adrian. So fucking good."

He'd never been a quiet lover, always intent on showing just how good it did feel. Dropping a hand to his cock, he twined his fingers with Adrian's, stroking their hands over his cock, breath hard and panting. "Fuck, fuck, fuck," he chanted breathlessly. "Don't stop, Adrian. Don't fucking stop."

Each sound between them only increased their enjoyment of the act. The hard drive of Adrian's body repeatedly drove deep into Jamie until the unbearable need for release began to take them over. The slap of their flesh was pure music.

With each thrust, his hand ran over Jamie's cock. Leaning over, his teeth caught at the edge of Jamie's shoulder. The heat of his ragged breath fanned over Jamie's skin as he grunted with the harder exertion to reach his own climax.

Jamie shuddered hard, meeting every thrust as he fucked himself on Adrian's cock, his own prick sliding through the tunnel of their fingers. Forehead pressing against the wall, he grunted and moaned, the sounds long and deep as he came, ass clenching tight around Adrian's cock as he shot onto the wall and floor beneath them.

The jerk of Adrian's hips buried him tightly

within Jamie as he came. A muffled cry escaped him; his head turned and his teeth closed around Jamie's skin. As his body shuddered hard in its pleasure, his breath froze in his throat.

When he could regain his breath, his body pinned Jamie's to the wall as he leaned heavily into him.

"Damn," Jamie mumbled. "You're makin' me feel old, pretty boy. But Lord, what a way to go."

A lazy chuckle sounded near Jamie's ear. "Guess that rules out another go?"

"Lord, Lord, Lord," Jamie laughed, shaking his head. "Been a long time for this cowboy, kid. I'm thinkin' food." He groaned as he shifted, Adrian's cock sliding out of him slowly. Turning around, Jamie fell back against the wall, an arm wrapping around Adrian to reel him in for a slow, easy kiss. "Makin' me feel young again."

Giving Jamie a curious look as he responded to the kiss with a slow brush of his lips, Adrian asked, "How old are you anyway?"

"Thirty-two," Jamie murmured. "You? Lord, please tell me you're over eighteen."

"Told you before. I'm twenty-four. Did you forget in the heat of the moment?" Adrian's tone sounded faintly teasing.

Jamie chuckled and rolled his eyes. "You fried my brain, pretty boy. You hungry? There's a damn good steakhouse not far from here, 'bout halfway to my place."

Adrian didn't seem to be the least bit self conscious leaning against the complete stranger he'd just fucked. Slowly pulling away, he said, "I need to take a piss first. If you'd point to your bathroom. Then I'll think about food."

Peeling the condom off, he looked for the nearest trash can before he tossed the rubber into it.

"Through there," Jamie said, pointing to a doorway behind Adrian. "Through that door, and second door on the right down the hallway." He bent to pull his jeans and underwear back up, wiping himself off before tucking back in. "Dinner's on me, if ya want."

Gathering up his clothes, Adrian headed for the bathroom. He wasn't gone more than a few minutes before the bathroom door opened and he stepped out. He looked a bit more rumpled than when he'd first entered the place. "I can follow behind you in my car. A free steak dinner sounds great to me."

"Excellent!" Jamie grinned and started putting his tools away, making sure the soldering gun was cool before setting it back in its stand. When he was done, he draped a white cloth over the glass on his worktable, grabbed his hat, and settled it on his head. "Ready? I'm in the dark blue pickup."

Nodding to him, Adrian stuffed his hands into his pockets as he moved towards the door, following behind Jamie.

PART TWO

When Adrian entered the store, he looked around for Jamie, but nobody was manning the counter. He could hear the strains of a country and western song coming from the back room. Some guy singing about how his girlfriend thought his tractor was sexy or something like that. Just the sound made Adrian pause and he tried not to laugh. The concept was well beyond him.

Finally he moved towards the back and stopped in the doorway. Jamie was in front of his work bench, fine ass swaying as he worked on a glass pattern. Not saying anything, Adrian just watched the tightly denim encased movement and felt a rising response from himself.

All Adrian had to do was look at the damn man, and he was hard in an instant.

Fully engrossed in his work, Jamie went from humming along to full-out singing, carrying a tune better than most cowboys could claim. With the precision of a surgeon, he began cutting, drawing the glasscutter along the serpentine lines of the pattern.

The urge to touch and taste was simply there all of a sudden, and it pushed Adrian forward towards the cowboy. His gaze roamed freely over Jamie, damn near entranced. He had to stop just short of him, not wanting to startle him into ruining the glass. Quietly, he cleared his throat to let Jamie know he was there.

The smooth motion of the blade over glass

stopped and Jamie looked over his shoulder. The smile was immediate. "Hey, gorgeous! You just get here?"

"Yeah. I thought I'd drop by and see what you were up to." Standing beside Jamie, he eyed the work laid out on the table. To say Jamie had talent would be an understatement. Even the small piece he'd been working showed a great deal of skill and talented flair.

Jamie's gaze ran over Adrian like a slow caress. "Gimme 'bout two minutes and a kiss hello and I'll be up for anything," he drawled, voice thick and deep.

"Not so surprisingly, I'm already up." Nudging against Jamie, Adrian crowded him slightly to shift the cowboy's position to face him better. Before anything else could be said, he leaned towards Jamie, his lips molding to his, and a hungry tongue probed between them.

Jamie's soft chuckle filled the kiss before fading into a moan. The glasscutter dropped to the wooden worktable and Jamie's fingers were sliding through Adrian's hair, tilting his head just enough to deepen the kiss. When they finally came up for air, he grinned.

"Now...I'm up." He pressed his hips forward, pushing their denim-covered cocks together.

Adrian's hand slipped between them to run his fingers over the outline of Jamie's cock. Rubbing gently against the material, he grinned. "Hmm...I'm thinking we're just going to have to do something about that. As soon as you get done with work."

"Lemme go flip the sign, lock the door, and you can have your way with me." Giving Adrian a quick wink and a kiss, Jamie hurried to close up shop.

Leaning back against the table, Adrian folded his arms across his chest and waited for the cowboy. Visions were already playing havoc in his head, and he had one hell of an itch that he wanted scratched.

Jamie returned a few seconds later, minus a shirt but still wearing his trademark black cowboy hat. Stopping just in the doorway to the workroom, he hooked his thumbs in the belt loops of his faded jeans, hips cocked as he smirked over at Adrian.

Licking his lips, he said, "You've got a cowboy wantin' a ride, babe."

A slow downward sweep of his gaze took Jamie in and an appreciative half smile curved Adrian's lip. "Think the table is comfortable enough for that?"

"Got somethin' better." Jamie sauntered past Adrian, hips swaying just slightly. In one corner of the workroom, he drew back a curtain, revealing a tattered but comfortable-looking sofa. "Have a seat, pretty boy. I wanna ride that sweet cock."

"It works absolutely perfectly for me." Unfastening his shirt, Adrian slipped it off and tossed it on the table before he took off his shoes.

As Adrian undressed, Jamie walked over to one of the cabinets and rummaged through it, finally pulling out a small square package and tube of gel. He tossed both onto the couch, stripped down, and shoved a naked Adrian down onto the seat.

"Been wantin' this," he said, straddling Adrian's lap.

"You have, have you?" Chuckling, Adrian stretched leisurely beneath him, the upward push of his body grinding to Jamie's ass. Both of his hands settled on the cowboy's hips, pressing him down against the movement. "Don't think I've thought about much except the feel of your sweet ass myself."

Jamie hummed, hands on the sofa as he ground down against Adrian. "Then show me, pretty boy."

Finding the wrapped condom near them, Adrian tore it open and quickly sheathed his cock in the rubber. As he slicked the lube over it, he eyed Jamie with a grin. "You're about to be shown."

Using his hand to guide the movement, the other shifted Jamie slightly before Adrian quickly impaled him. Without giving the cowboy a chance for a breath, Adrian slid home deep inside him.

"Oh, sweet fuck..." Jamie groaned, fingers digging into Adrian's chest, ass squeezing his cock. "God, Adrian, feels so fucking good."

Impatient to feel far more, Adrian's thrust began at a fast rhythm, pushing in against the tightness around his cock. "Incredible, fucking incredible, Jamie." The quickening rhythm of his breathing matched the beat of Adrian's heart as his body felt the buildup tighten inside him. "Fuck, I love this feeling."

Jamie was beyond speech, just moaning and panting and grunting, eyes alternating between wide open and closed. His fingers found their way to Adrian's nipples, taking them both and twisting them, pulling them. "Fuck me, baby. Come on, Adrian. Yeah...oh shit!" Jamie shouted and jerked, hips snapping as he shot over Adrian's stomach, his ass clamping tight.

With the pinch of the cowboy's fingers at his nipples, it took Adrian only two more hard thrusts before he came in Jamie's ass, feeling the contracting tightness milking his cock. It drew out the intensity of orgasm and had him groaning deeply, unable to speak or even so much as breathe.

"Mm..." Jamie hummed contentedly as they both came down. "Damn, that was fucking awesome, baby."

Slipping his arms around Jamie, Adrian drew the cowboy down to relax against him. Turning his head slightly, Adrian nuzzled in against his hair. "I was thinking of repeat performances after some dinner. I know a place. Probably not your style but the food is damn good. It's on the corner of fifth and Aston." Nipping lightly at Jamie's ear, he nibbled on him before letting go. With a groan, he withdrew from the cowboy and stood up. Unrolling the rubber, he dropped it into the trash and grabbed one of the clean rags nearby. After wiping off, he tossed it to Jamie.

Jamie shrugged as he cleaned off. "Long as they got beer, I'm game for anything, babe." He grinned and dropped the rag onto the couch before standing and getting dressed.

Putting his jeans and shirt back on, Adrian turned to look at him as he slid back into his shoes. "Oh, it has beer..."

Lifting an eyebrow quizzically, Jamie said, "O...kay... Why do I have the feeling there's going to be a nice little culture shock?"

"It's just a place where a lot of my friends hang out, Jamie." Adrian grinned as he fished his keys out of his pocket. "At least you'll like the food."

Jamie chuckled as he sat down to tug on his

boots. "Food's good." He stood and set his hat back in place, going from completely debauched to freshly fucked cowboy with a grin. "Company's better, though." He leaned for a quick kiss. "C'mon, babe. Let's go grab a bite."

"I'll agree with that." After giving Jamie a lingering kiss, Adrian sauntered casually through the store and outside to his car.

From the way Jamie kept eyeing him as he drove, Adrian figured the cowboy was already ready for round two. They just needed food first. Pulling up to the curb not too far away from the small club, Adrian turned off the car and laid his hand teasingly on Jamie's thigh. "There it is. Just up ahead."

The club front was sandwiched between a New Age shop and a building with a sign that proclaimed *The Church of Divine Thought*. The whole area seemed somewhat rundown and ramshackle.

Jamie blinked as he stared out the windshield. "Oh, now this is gonna be interestin'."

"Time for a different taste, lover." Chuckling, Adrian ran his hand upward along Jamie's thigh before squeezing lightly at his crotch. "Then it'll be dessert time."

Sliding out of the car, he waited until Jamie got out, then led him into the club. Stepping into the place was like stepping into the past. Several groups were clustered around individual tables in the dark, smoky atmosphere. No neon signs flashed, announcing the latest beer; instead, hand-written signs hung on the wall, advertising the menu and bar selection.

The crowd was comprised of a range of people-from hippy to beatnik, and the décor reflected it. Some of the best gaudiness of the fifties and sixties had found a home in the form of lava lamp centerpieces on the tables to one wall draped in what looked like one huge piece of black velvet.

"Damn." Eyes wide to take it all in, Jamie followed Adrian through the club toward one of the tables. As they sat down, a young man, practically draped in black, walked up to them. Pierced from eyebrow to God knows where, a number of tattoos were just barely visible beneath the tight black t-shirt.

"Where have you been hiding?" the young man asked Adrian as he flipped open a small notepad.

"Just been working, Izzy. You seen Lucy or Nostradamus in today?" Adrian asked as he pulled one of the chairs out and sat down.

"Nope, not yet. If you want dinner, it'll be a few minutes. Suzy had Claude trying to contact her grandfather, but he ended up channeling some old guy from, like, 1631. He should be out of it in a bit."

"Not a problem. We'll take a couple of blue balls while we're waiting." Glancing over at Jamie, he asked, "You want a steak or burger?"

Jamie just stared at him, mouth open. Finally reeling his thoughts back into some sort of order, he said, "Burger." When the waiter left, Jamie just had to ask. "Blue balls? That's the last thing I'd expect to get from you."

"Claude was being a smart ass when he named it. Said he got horny as hell after he taste tested five glasses of it, but he couldn't do a damn thing about it since he was tending the bar at the same time. Couldn't even talk Suzy into giving him a blow job behind the counter. Just about everybody here that night caught onto his problem and did their best to make it worse." Adrian was fully aware his friends were slightly off the scale of the one to ten factor.

"I take it a 'blue ball' is some sort of bizarre alcoholic concoction," Jamie chuckled. As if in answer, Izzy returned a moment later, setting two glasses of unnatural blue...stuff...on the table. Jamie just...stared at it. "It looks like antifreeze, Adrian. Only blue."

"Enjoy, guys. Claude's back at the stove and your burger and steak will be right up."

"Thanks, Izzy." Adrian smirked as he picked up the tall, frosted glass. "Just take a drink, Jamie. It might not be as bizarre as you think."

With a laugh, Izzy headed back towards the kitchen.

Jamie looked skeptical, but he finally just swallowed his doubts and took a sip. "Whoa. That's...uh...strong."

"Better than the piss water served at most places." Adrian took a healthy swallow and gave Jamie a wide grin. "If you don't like it, you can get something else."

"Actually..." Jamie took another drink, this one less tentative. "It's quite good, babe."

Suddenly a dead silence fell over the entire club. Adrian raised a finger to his lips as he looked at Jamie. Not even the sound of cutlery rattling against dinner plates intruded.

A young couple took center stage in the room. The man sat on the floor, placing his bongo drums in front of him. A stool was taken from the bar for the young woman, and she sat, straddling the wooden slates. "Life."

To the accompaniment of the rhythm of the drum, she spoke. "One pack of Camels. Bleeding heart tonight. Smoke, my only company. Love. Oh, not tonight. No heart to touch. No soul to care."

A chill crawled up Jamie's spine and he shivered slightly, gaze riveted to the poet. Adrian listened silently to her, caught by the cadence of words and the message beneath.

"Tomorrow night. Over again. Surrounded in smoky haze. Still bleeding. The stars above, the same darkness. Inside." As she bowed her head, long black hair spilling over her shoulders, the crowd began to snap their fingers.

It took a moment for Jamie to realize that was their form of applause. Following Adrian's example, he snapped his fingers as well, brain still reeling from the poem. For something so simple, it had been anything but.

When the woman and man stood, normal sounds resumed around the club. Adrian smiled at Jamie. "Amanda's great, isn't she? I think that's what I love about her style. It's made up as she sits there; it's from inside her without real time to think."

Finally finding his voice, Jamie said, "I'm speechless."

"That's the only one she'll do tonight. We're lucky we made it in time to hear her." Adrian leaned back in his chair as a man bustled to the table, carrying their plates. "Hey, Claude."

Claude set Jamie's plate in front of him, loaded with a humongous hamburger and fries before he placed Adrian's in front of him. "Your usual, kid, and I got a message from your mama. She's been trying to get through. Very worried about you."

"She knows I'm fine." Reaching for his fork and knife, Adrian began cutting the meat on his plate.

"You know she doesn't like DeSalvo." Claude quickly shot the comment at Adrian before he turned to eye Jamie. "And who is this?"

"This is Jamie Holland. Jamie, this is Claude Gardner. The chef and owner of this place."

"How d'ya do," Jamie said with a nod, reaching out to shake Claude's hand. "Excellent place you got here."

Claude smiled proudly as he shook Jamie's hand. "I hope you're enjoying the in-house beer. Made it myself."

"Hey, Claude, Upton's here with the order!" Izzy yelled from the kitchen.

Muttering, Claude added, "I'll have to tell you the story sometime when I'm not so busy." Whirling around, his tone rose as he strode back to the kitchen. "Am I the only one that works around here?"

Laughing, Adrian continued digging into his mushroom and onion smothered steak. "He does tell the story better than I do."

Jamie grinned and, looking down at the size of his burger, said, "Now this is worthy of a Texan."

"So what's the size of a Texan burger?" With a grin, Adrian just had to ask.

"Big," Jamie said, dumping a puddle of ketchup on his plate. Scooping up some with a fry, his grin turned wicked. "Didn't you know, babe? Everything's big in Texas."

Adrian's lips twitched before he started laughing. "Must be true since they made you."

Jamie just winked before doing lewd things to the French fry.

Watching the lick of Jamie's tongue got Adrian all hot and bothered. In his case, it wasn't that hard to do. "Keep it up and you won't be finishing that burger, Jamie."

Jamie's gaze fastened on Adrian as he deep throated the fry. Then he pulled it back out, lips wrapping around it, sucking away the ketchup. Somewhere nearby, a fork clattered onto a plate.

Continuing to eat his steak and baked potato, Adrian figured he'd better fortify himself for the night ahead. His eyes never left Jamie, though he hadn't squirmed in his chair, yet. An appreciative murmur came from his left, and Adrian looked over to see one of his friends grinning like a madman at him.

"Mind your own business, Nero."

Nero blew Adrian a kiss before returning to his own meal.

Jamie chuckled and dutifully finished his dinner. And although he refrained from any further questionable acts with his food, he did rest his foot on the chair between Adrian's thighs, pressing the toe of his boot against Adrian's crotch.

Reminded throughout the meal of the state of his own body, Adrian made quick work of the steak and paid little attention to the rest of the club's show. When they were done, he pulled out his wallet and slapped a twenty on the table as his head jerked towards the door. Clearly, it was time to leave.

Tossing back the last of his beer, Jamie stood, licking his lips. He followed Adrian outside and as they neared the car, he said, "You look...hot and bothered, babe."

"You're gonna find out real soon, cowboy." Adrian smirked at him before he slid into the drivers' side of the car. After Jamie got in, Adrian's hand rested on his upper thigh. "We're heading to my apartment. I can take you back to your shop later on tonight so you can get your truck."

"Just get me somewhere so I can swallow that sweet cock of yours."

"Fuck, Jamie. Damn good thing I only live a couple of blocks from this place, or you'd be busy right now." Letting go of Jamie's leg to start the car, the hand returned to his thigh as Adrian pulled out into a lull in the traffic.

"Doin' what, babe?" Jamie asked, sliding a hand up Adrian's thigh, squeezing the hardening bulge in his jeans. "Slidin' my lips up and down that thick cock? Pushing my tongue into the slit?"

Adrian didn't need a wild imagination because he already knew what Jamie's mouth would feel like. Only directing one telling look at the cowboy, Adrian focused on the street until they pulled up in front of his building. After he turned off the car, he grabbed Jamie's hand, pressing it tighter to the denim. "Let's decide if my cock wants your mouth or ass when we get inside."

"Mmm, let's do that." Jamie just grinned and unbuckled, then got out as quickly as possible. He started up the steps, jeans tight across a firm ass.

Thankfully nobody was hanging around the

hallway to bother Adrian since he was more intent on getting into his own apartment. Moving past Jamie, he reached the front door and unlocked it. Walking inside, he tossed his key towards the counter near the kitchen and quickly shut the door behind Jamie once he was inside.

"Get the hell out of your clothes, cowboy."

Jamie didn't bat an eye, just turned and started for the bedroom, shirt falling to the floor as he went. When he reached the doorway, he toed his boots off and undid his jeans, shoving them down. Then he turned to Adrian and spread out his arms.

"Come an' get me."

By the time Jamie turned around, Adrian had already stripped naked. As he walked towards the cowboy, once he was close enough, the movement of his body pushed Jamie through the doorway and into the bedroom. One hand slid between them, covering both of their cocks, and began a slow, leisurely tug over them. "You hungry at all, old man?"

Jamie's back hit the opposite wall and he draped his arms over Adrian's shoulders, hips rocking as he pushed into the strokes. "Mm, always," he rumbled. "Fuck, your hand feels good. Yeah…"

"If that feels good, then how about this…" Trailing off, Adrian dropped to his knees, letting his mouth take over for his hand. His tongue teased against the slit of Jamie's cock, licking at the drops before his lips encircled the head, pulling the cowboy's length deep into his mouth.

"Oh, sweet fuck…" Jamie moaned, fingers sliding through Adrian's hair. "God, yes…right there, baby...fuck." Holding onto Adrian's head, Jamie thrust his hips forward, groaning as he slid into the slick heat of Adrian's mouth.

Adrian's throat relaxed, taking him fully in as his hand played beneath Jamie's balls, one finger teasing along the crack of his ass. Slowly, Adrian worked him, keeping Jamie close to the fevered pitch of need with the glide of his tongue and teeth. His other hand lowered to his lap, the slow jerk of motion over his own cock increasing the slow, burning fire.

"Adrian." Jamie's hold tightened, movements quickening. "Don't stop, baby..."

After a moment more, Adrian finally slowly pulled back. "On the bed, cowboy. The lube is in the drawer next to the bed. I want you ready for me."

Groaning, it took Jamie a few seconds to collect his wits. He tugged the drawer open, grabbed the lube, and dropped onto the bed, legs spreading wide. Slicking two fingers, he wasted no time, staring at Adrian as he pushed both deep inside himself.

His gaze never left the cowboy as he walked around to get a condom from the stand. A near painful throb raced outward from his cock as he watched Jamie's fingers fucking his own tight hole. Taking the lube, he poured some out and ran his hand over the rubber. Once ready, Adrian moved to the end of the bed and slid in between Jamie's legs.

Hooking his arms under Jamie's legs, he drew them up to his shoulders, raising the cowboy's ass off the bed. At the perfect level, it only took one slow movement to penetrate him.

"Oh, fuck..." The words were drawn out, Jaime's eyes going wide as he stared up at Adrian.

"Deep...so deep, Adrian..."

"How I want to take you, babe." Several times, he thrust with an exquisite slowness, feeling Jamie's ass taking in every inch. The haze spread outward through Adrian's body as he gripped tightly to Jamie's upper thighs, holding him in place. "Use your hand on yourself. I'm gonna watch you fall apart for me."

Jamie nodded and licked his bottom lip, fingers wrapping around his cock. He took the strokes slow and long, head tilting back with a groan. "Adrian..."

Driving as deep as he could possibly go, Adrian felt the tight inner contractions of Jamie's ass. Changing the speed, he quickened the motion in a more brutal pace, the slap of their skin echoing the rhythm. A low guttural grunt escaped Adrian with the harder exertion, leaving him barely hanging onto his own control of himself.

"Fuck." Jamie hissed, fist jerking wildly. "Adrian!" Hips snapping up, Jamie shot over his chest and stomach, ass clenching tight around Adrian's cock.

"Oh yeah, that's what I needed to see." Adrian drank in the sight of his lover with an intense pleasure. Each push of his hips slid against the tight muscles until it sent Adrian over the edge as well. The hard strain of his body locked to Jamie in a shuddering release.

Panting and slick with come and sweat, Jamie simply melted into the bed, releasing his cock and letting his arm fall to the side as they both started to come back down to Earth. "Damn, baby. That was..." He shook his head, still working to catch his breath.

As Adrian carefully pulled Jamie's legs back to the bed, he leaned down, licking at the sweet taste, cleaning the cowboy off. When Adrian finished, he tugged the rubber off, aimed for the trash, then collapsed beside him. "Intense? One hell of a rush? God, it was a kick being in you that deep. That has got to happen more often."

"Baby...I'd do anything to get you that deep," Jamie chuckled. He rolled onto his side and nestled up against Adrian, dropping a quick kiss to his chest. "Anything at all."

PART THREE

The first chance he got, Adrian picked up the phone, dialing Jamie's number. The cowboy had given it to him before Adrian had left the restaurant, and he'd promised he'd call Jamie when he could. Adrian had a few minutes before he had to be out the door, and his foot tapped impatiently as he waited for Jamie to answer.

"Hello?"

"Jamie, it's Adrian. Thought I'd give you a call and see what you're up to."

"Oh! Hi there, pretty boy."

Adrian heard the click of a lighter and an indrawn breath before Jamie continued, "Just got out of the shower, actually. What's up, sexy?"

"I wanted to know if you were in the mood for dinner or something tomorrow night." Adrian sounded very casual even as his mind envisioned thoughts of a lean, lanky body stepping out of the shower. Sometimes it was hard to focus when those kind of images intruded.

"Hold on a sec."

Adrian settled on the edge of his bed, putting on his shoes as he listened to the sounds of Jamie moving around.

"Okay. That's better. Sorry, had to get my sweats on. Dinner sounds great. What time?"

Chuckling, Adrian said, "Thanks for the visuals. I've already got a hard on. Looks like I'm stuck taking care of it myself tonight." He had no problem giving Jamie some good visuals as well. "You can come over to the apartment tomorrow. Say about five or so. Sound good?"

"Five sounds good." A few seconds passed and Jamie chuckled. "A hard-on, huh? Guess it doesn't help to mention that I stroked myself off in the shower, thinking about your cock up my ass."

"Smart ass." Adrian couldn't help laughing. "I have to be out the door in five minutes, and you just made it harder to do that." As tempted as he was, Adrian didn't have time for phone sex. "Guess you'll just have to dream about it until tomorrow night."

A soft groan came through the receiver then. "Mm, too late, pretty boy," Jamie murmured.

Adrian's imagination kicked into vivid overtime, knowing exactly what Jamie was doing. His body tightened with the thought, and he had to shift on the bed. "Fuck, Jamie. I need a taste of that."

"Mm," Jamie moaned softly. A sucking sound followed, Jamie's breath hitching slightly. "Tastes good, pretty boy. Salty-sweet."

He knew Jamie was playing him. It didn't help he'd had no relief in almost a week. His tone came out slightly gruff. "You realize tomorrow night, you're gonna pay for this."

Adrian heard the slight catch in Jamie's breath before the cowboy moaned, the sound forming Adrian's name. A moment later, he chuckled softly. "I'm counting on it."

The sounds told him Jamie had indeed come. Tension vibrated through him, and there wasn't a damn thing Adrian could do. In fact, he wouldn't do anything about it all until he saw Jamie. Murmuring softly, his voice carried a husky overtone. "Just remember, I'm not getting any relief until I see you."

"I know. And I'm going to enjoy every second of it."

"Tomorrow at five, Jamie." Chuckling, he hung up the phone.

* * * *

Adrian had been trying to get ready for the *date* he'd set with Jamie. Hearing a knock at the door, he headed towards the living room and opened the door. Seeing his cousin, Lucy, he took hold of her arm and pulled her inside. Once the door was shut, he said, "Lucy, I need that diamond I gave you yesterday."

Giving him an indignant look, she pulled her arm away from him, "You didn't give me a diamond."

Sighing, he carefully explained, "You remember that pretty pink stone you wanted to keep for me?"

It took her a moment to realize what Adrian was talking about. "Oh, yeah, that. It was so pretty. But it doesn't skip very well."

"Skip?" Almost afraid to ask, Adrian did anyway.

Lucy smiled at him before she headed to the couch and sat down. Adrian always kept interesting pieces of glass and stone arrayed on the coffee table to amuse her. "In the fountain. But the white stone I had skipped a lot better than that pink one."

Trying to swallow the rising tide of panic, Adrian managed not to strangle Lucy and asked calmly, "What fountain, Lucy?"

Without a care in the world, she answered.

"Staunton."

"Shit!" Adrian muttered under his breath. When another knock sounded at the door, he wrenched it open.

Jamie gave him a surprised look. "Not ready yet?"

Stepping aside to let him in, Adrian gave him a harried look. "It'll only take me a minute or two to finish dressing."

As Adrian disappeared back in the direction of his bedroom, Jamie eyed Lucy. "Hello, Miss Lucy."

"Pretty cowboy." Lucy seemed delighted to see Jamie as she jumped from the couch and made a beeline to him. Quickly smothering him in a tight hug, she smiled happily at him.

Bemused, Jamie returned the hug before she wandered off back to her stones.

"Baxter wants to know how old you are, Jamie." Tilting her head slightly as if listening to something, she nodded a bit before she continued. "He also says he wants a hat just like yours."

"Thirty-two." Jamie answered her promptly. No more than amused by her translating for her 'rabbit friend', he easily humored the young girl. "I'll see if I can find one for him."

"Oh, would you?" The promise was enough to bring a brilliant smile to her lips as she looked up at him.

"Would he what?" When Adrian returned to the living room, he wanted to know what Lucy was trying to rope Jamie into doing.

"Baxter wants a hat like Jamie's."

"I'll see how much one costs, Lucy." Adrian was

long used to indulging his cousin. "You gonna stay here for now or head home."

"I want to play with your stones, Adrian. Besides Nostradamus won't be home for another hour."

The look Jamie gave Adrian seem to ask, *Nostradamus?*

Adrian just shook his head. "Never mind, Jamie. We need to stop off at the Staunton before we go out. We can take my car."

"Staunton?"

"Long story." As they headed out the door, Adrian filled him in on as few of the details as he could get away with.

* * * *

The sound of the water from the fountain made Adrian need to take a piss. But right now that was the least of his worries. He'd left Jamie in the car and probably didn't have much time to find the diamond. After slowly circling the perimeter of the fountain, Adrian dropped his pack on the ledge. As he fished through it for a flashlight, he was startled by the sound of Jamie's voice.

"What the hell are you doing?"

Adrian knew he could either explain or brush it off and go back to the car. But then he would have to return later to find the damn diamond. Opting for the former as being easier, Adrian tried to explain, "Lucy took a liking to one of my stones, and I let her play with it. She skipped one of my diamonds in the fountain, and now, I need to find it."

"A diamond?" Looking somewhat incredulous, Jamie's gaze drifted between the fountain and Adrian.

"A pink diamond. A large, pink diamond." Hurriedly he handed a flashlight to Jamie before he dug out another one for himself and flicked it on. "I've got to find that damn diamond, Jamie." He fully expected the cowboy to join him in the search of the fountain.

Taking the flashlight, Jamie just shook his head. "I'm still trying to figure out how the hell you lose a rock that big."

"Told you. Lucy saw the damn thing and wanted to play with it. I didn't think she would try to skip it in this damn fountain."

Jamie walked around the perimeter of the massive stone fountain, shining the light here and there in the water. Then he grumbled. "We aren't going to find anything like this.

Watching Jamie for a moment, Adrian gave him an irritated look as he slipped off his shoes. "We're going to have to go into the fountain. Nobody is around to see us."

Gingerly, Adrian stepped into the water. Feeling the water seep into the legs of his pants, he muttered, "Fuck, that's cold."

Jamie's mouth dropped open and for a minute, he just stared wide-eyed at Adrian. "That's it. It's official. You're insane."

He hopped on one foot, then the other, tugging off his cowboy boots. With a grumble, he stepped into the fountain, shooting a glare at Adrian—for the cold, for losing the damn diamond, for this whole absurd situation. "If I wanted to go swimmin'," he muttered as he walked through the shin-high water, "I'd have gone home and jumped into the pool."

"We just need to find the damn diamond." Carefully his hand swept back and forth, lighting the area as Adrian searched the water for the sparkle of a diamond.

"Don't suppose makin' one out of glass is an option," Jamie said as he continued his own search. He passed by Adrian, each of them going the opposite direction, and reached out, brushing his fingers across Adrian's chest. "We'll find it."

The glass comment earned Jamie a disgruntled look from Adrian. "If I thought it would fool Eric, I'd do it, but it won't, so I won't."

With the touch, Adrian paused, trying not to laugh. "Only you would want to fuck when we're ass deep in cold water."

"We're not ass-deep; we're knee-deep. And who said I want to fuck?" Jamie's grin didn't exactly reflect the denial, but he just winked before moving on.

"Fucking smart ass." Ignoring his companion, Adrian continued his slow, methodical search of the water. "Maybe one of us will step on the damn thing."

The sound of someone clearing their throat made Adrian lift his head. As he raised the flash light, the beam caught the badge of the cop watching them.

"Now there's a hard-on killer," Jamie muttered. "Evenin', Officer." Jamie tipped his Stetson at the cop.

Swallowing hard, Adrian managed to say, "Hello, Officer."

"Mind telling me what you two fellows are doing in the fountain?"

Thinking fast, Adrian's hand slipped into his back pocket, taking out his wallet. As he leaned over towards the water, he dropped the wallet into it. "This idiot tossed my wallet into the fountain, and we're trying to find it now."

"Shouldn't have been arguing 'bout dinner," Jamie shot back under his breath, but loud enough for the cop to hear. "Hey. That it?" He shined his light near Adrian's right foot.

"Well, now that you've found it," the officer said, "don't you think it's time to get out?" An eyebrow lifted, more in warning than amusement.

Hastily grabbing his now wet wallet, Adrian quickly moved to the edge of the fountain. "No problem, Officer. Sorry about this."

He didn't want to get out, but he had no choice. Picking his shoes up, he told the cop, "We'll be out of your way now."

"You do that." The cop gave them both a nod as Jamie stooped like he was scratching his foot before walking through the water to the edge.

"Thank you, Officer," he said as he stepped out. Once the cop was gone, Jamie turned to Adrian, grabbing an arm and jerking him close, wet clothes and all. "You owe me." He pressed something cold and hard in Adrian's hand.

Relief flooded Adrian as he felt the chill stone in his stone. His fingers wrapped tightly around it as his arm slide around Jamie. "I owe you a hell of a lot."

"Uh-huh." Jamie grinned and tipped his hat back just enough to lean close for a kiss. "But I ain't collectin' here. It's cold. Where to?"

"Anywhere but here. That cop will be coming back, and it's fucking cold now." Shivering slightly, he returned the kiss before pulling away from Jamie. "We both need to dry our clothes."

Stuffing the diamond into the vial he'd pulled from his pocket, Adrian headed back to the car.

Jamie grimaced as he slid into the passenger's seat of Adrian's car. Their jeans were cold and clammy from above the knees and down. As Adrian started the car, Jamie turned the heat on full-blast, directing it to the floorboard vents in hopes of drying out their jeans.

"I vote we go back to my place, change clothes, and go out to eat. There's a great little steakhouse 'bout three miles from the house — great steaks, great music, great dance floor."

With no traffic around, Adrian quickly pulled out of the parking space. A vague complaint colored his tone as he muttered, "It's warm enough without the heat."

Quickly rolling down the car window, he added. "I vote for that. I'm fucking starving."

Jamie just rolled his eyes, not bothering to turn off the heat. "Tryin' to dry out our jeans. Yeah. I could definitely go for a nice juicy steak and some good ol' dancin'. Maybe I can even talk a certain someone into a buckle-polisher or two?"

Pausing at a stop light, Adrian gave him a blank look. "What the hell is that?"

Jamie blinked. "Buckle-polisher. Brooks and Dunn's 'Neon Moon'?" He lifted an eyebrow at Adrian. "A slow song. You know...rubbing, belt buckle-polishing?"

"Brooks and Dunn?" Blinking, he just shook his head before accelerating the car when the light turned green. He looked completely clueless. "You know, I hate dancing."

"You need some culture, kid," Jamie snorted. "Dancin's good for ya. Helps circulate the blood, work off the food. Damn good exercise."

"So is sex, and it's a hell of a lot more enjoyable." Adrian smirked at him as he laid his hand on Jamie's thigh. Pulling into the parking garage of the apartment building, Adrian turned off the car. With another smirk, he squeezed Jamie's thigh before releasing him and getting out of the car.

Jamie chuckled as he got out, digging into his jeans pocket for his keys. "Think of dancin' as foreplay. Gettin' all hot and bothered out there, not able to do a damn thing 'bout it." He gave Adrian a wink before starting up the outside stairs leading to the second floor.

Following behind him, Adrian muttered, "That is not my idea of a good time. Throwing you on the bed, and fucking your brains out is my idea of a good time."

Adrian's gaze slid down to the tightly encased ass in front of him, and he murmured, "Oh, hell yeah."

Jamie stopped at the top of the stairs, causing Adrian to run right into him. "Uh-huh," he murmured, turning his head just enough to see Adrian. He licked his lips and flashed Adrian a wicked grin. "Thought you were starving, hot shot."

When he ran into him, Adrian deliberately took advantage of it. His hand cupped against Jamie's ass, slowly rubbing over him. "If you didn't have such a great ass, I wouldn't look, now would I?"

"Mm," Jamie hummed softly. "Damn tease is what you are." He wiggled a bit, just enough to graze his butt over Adrian's crotch, then he started down the short walkway to his apartment door.

When Jamie walked off, Adrian muttered, "And you call me a tease. Yeah, right."

Getting the door open, Jamie walked inside, tossing his keys onto the bar.

Entering the apartment behind him, Adrian immediately dropped his shoes and began stripping off his wet pants. The stickiness plastered to his skin, leaving an uncomfortable feeling.

Before Adrian even halfway undressed, Jamie walked down the hall, naked ass swaying just a bit as he whistled a country song on the way to the bathroom.

Adrian's appreciative gaze followed Jamie. The sight of him naked except for his cowboy hat had his full interest. Knowing they'd never get out of the door if he tried to take a shower with Jamie, he headed for the pantry to toss his pants into the dryer. Five minutes later, Adrian was in and out of the half bath, freshly showered.

A few minutes later, Jamie emerged from the hall bathroom, towel tucked around his waist. He leaned against the bedroom door frame, hat dangling from his fingertips as he stared at Adrian. When Adrian's towel dropped to the floor, Jamie gave a low, appreciative whistle. "Now that's a sight to drag any cowboy from Texas."

Feeling Jamie's gaze on him and hearing the

whistle, Adrian couldn't resist the urge to flex for him. Turning his head to look back at him, he bent slightly over the dresser to pick up his shirt.

"Oh. Yeah. You are a definite tease." Jamie tossed his hat onto the bed and came up behind Adrian, sliding his fingertips down Adrian's spine as he pressed up against him. "You know," he murmured, lips following the path of his fingers, "we are never going to get out of here."

Enjoying the feel of Jamie, Adrian leaned back against him for a moment before he deliberately pulled away. Quickly slipping his shirt on, he said, "Oh yeah we will. I'm starving. And we have plenty of time for the best fun."

With a groan, Jamie landed a smack to Adrian's ass before pulling out clothes for himself. It took him a few minutes, but he finally managed to pour himself into the dark jeans. As Jamie dressed, Adrian got his pants from the dryer and finished dressing.

Jamie slipped on a dark blue flannel shirt, leaving it unbuttoned as he sat down to put on his socks and boots. "Hair up or down?" he asked, scrutinizing himself in the mirror.

Leaning against the dresser, Adrian eyed him. "Umm, down. I love playing with your hair."

If he continued staring at Jamie much longer, they really wouldn't make it out the door. The sight of the cowboy was too damn enticing. Pushing from the dresser, Adrian left the room. Near the front door, he bent over to put on his sneakers.

Chuckling, Jamie shook his head. Popping his hat back on, he opted to leave his hair loose this time. As he left the bedroom, he buttoned up his shirt.

"Ready?" He grabbed his keys and wallet from the bar, shoving his wallet into his back pocket. "Let's take the truck. Haven't driven her in a few days."

"I was going to suggest that since my seats are still probably wet. Lead the way." He moved up behind Jamie and playfully leered at him.

He glanced at Adrian over his shoulder. "Keep lookin' at me like that, and we won't be eatin'." He winked and waited until Adrian had the door closed and locked before leading the way back downstairs. "Mm. Yeah. Beer, steak, and dancin'. Sounds like my kind of evenin'."

"I'm in for the steak. Then I'm in for coming home and fucking you." He'd do his best to talk Jamie out of the rest of what he wanted to do. This time he kept his eyes on Jamie's back as he followed behind him down the stairs.

"C'mere," Jamie growled as he neared the truck. Leaning back against the driver's side door, he reached out and tugged Adrian close, his legs on either side of Adrian's thighs. "S'pose you could talk me out of dancin' if ya tried," he drawled, lips brushing over Adrian's as he hooked his fingers in the belt loops of Adrian's pants.

Adrian didn't resist the pull on him. His body found its own comfortable spot against Jamie as he raised his face, whispering to the press of Jamie's lips, "Depends on whether or not you bribe me into it."

"Mm...always bargainin'," Jamie murmured, tongue swiping slow across Adrian's lips. "Least I know how to bribe you." Giving Adrian a quick wink, Jamie groaned low, tongue pushing between

Adrian's lips.

The slow dart of his tongue greeted the probe of Jamie's. Adrian loved the way this man kissed, and each stroke from him encouraged a lingering kiss between them.

"Taste good," Jamie whispered into Adrian's mouth. "Taste like us." He sucked lightly on Adrian's tongue before pulling slowly away. "Food. Then home. I'm needin'."

"And what would you be needing, besides a steak?" With a bit of a smirk, Adrian pulled away before heading to the passenger side of the truck. Pulling open the door, he hopped in and buckled the seat belt.

"You. In my ass," Jamie grumbled as he climbed into the cab. After buckling, he started up the truck.

"Maybe a cold beer or two will cool you off."

"Food. Fucking." Jamie left it at that, and a few moments later he pulled into the parking lot for Rosie's Steakhouse. After shutting off the truck, he slid out of the cab and situated his hat better as he waited for Adrian.

Flashing him an arrogant 'I told you so' look, Adrian didn't look the least bit surprised Jamie was seeing things his way. "You do have to have priorities, Jamie. And if I weren't starving, it'd be fucking first."

Sliding out of the seat, he shut the door and headed towards the restaurant.

A few minutes later, they were seated in a booth with a good view of the dance floor. A trio played on the small stage, and Jamie was half-dancing, half-bouncing in his seat to the upbeat, twangy rhythm.

"What can I get ya boys?" The waitress flipped open a small pad and smiled at them both.

"Your twelve-ounce with baked potato and greens," Jamie said. "Oh! And a tall Coors."

"Same as him." Adrian eyed the wiggling body across from him. The music wasn't precisely his thing since he ignored country for the most part. He definitely preferred a heavier beat to his music.

As the waitress walked away, Jamie bit his bottom lip, eyeing the dance floor longingly. He simply couldn't sit still, fingers drumming on the wooden tabletop as he practically danced in the booth seat. The song was obviously one Jamie knew since he started humming along, singing a part here and there.

"You know I would dance with you if I knew how one danced to this. You can head over there if you want. There's more than one pair of eyes on you right now."

Jamie seemed iffy, but finally just leaned over the table for a quick kiss. "One song, then I'll be back." He slid out of the booth and out onto the dance floor, immediately joined by another man as they started dancing. There wasn't anything inherently sexual about it; just Jamie and the man laughing, both of them falling into a two-step in time with the music. Jamie's thumbs were tucked into the front pockets of his jeans, his steps easy and sure.

Adrian settled back in the booth, watching him with a faint smile. When the waitress brought their beers, he grabbed the bottle and took a drink.

After the song ended, Jamie and the man he'd been dancing with, clapped each other on the back, then went their separate ways. Jamie slid back into the booth, taking a healthy swallow of beer. "That was fun. You really should try it some time," he teased, a booted foot coming up to rest on the seat between Adrian's thighs.

Chuckling, he just shook his hand. "It's never been my ambition to learn that style of dance."

His hand rested on Jamie's ankle as he eyed him.

"Mm," Jamie purred, shifting lower in the seat until his foot was pressed to Adrian's crotch. "You definitely excel in more...primal forms."

"And that's exactly what will keep you satisfied, Jamie." Adrian had a rather smug air about him as he felt the slight pressure between his legs.

"Almost as much pride as a cowboy." Jamie gave him a teasing wink as the waitress returned with their food. Jamie took a deep breath, closing his eyes as the delicious smells hit him. "Mm. Smells damn good."

Settling back, he gave the waitress room to set down his plate. "Eat up, cowboy, cuz when we get home, I'll have dessert for you."

Jamie grinned at him around a mouthful of potato. "Adrian Cream Pie," he chuckled a minute later. He popped a piece of steak in his mouth and his eyes immediately closed, a soft sound escaping his lips as he looked like he was melting into the seat.

Cutting off several pieces of steak, Adrian began to eat as well. His nod was one of total agreement with Jamie.

Silence reigned as they both ate, and when Jamie finished, he settled back, a content grin on his lips. Pushing his plate away, he leaned back and grinned around the mouth of his beer bottle, tonguing the opening as he toyed with Adrian.

Adrian ate more slowly and only made it half way through his plate. His appetite wasn't nearly as large as Jamie's. Glancing up at him in the middle of taking a bite, Adrian watched the tongue action. "Is that a hint it's time to go home? Or do you want to dance some more?"

"Always ready when you are," Jamie said. With little regard for what others around them might think, he proceeded to tongue-fuck the beer bottle, grinning and moaning softly.

"Oh, I'm in no hurry, Jamie. You can dance some more if you want." Adrian managed to sound extremely casual as he ignored the tightening across the crotch of his pants.

Pressing his foot just a bit harder against Adrian, Jamie opened his mouth and slid his lips down the neck of the bottle. Pulling back up slowly, he flicked his tongue over the end. "Now, we can either stay," he said, "or we can go back to my place, and I can suck you dry."

"Just thought you wanted to dance some more is all." His eyes remained on Jamie as Adrian nonchalantly shrugged. Reaching into his back pocket, he went for his wallet but then realized he'd left it on the dresser to dry out.

Jamie slipped a few bills on the table, then stood. "I can think of other things," he said, the beer and need drawing out the words just a bit more than normal.

Sliding out of the booth, he stood up with Jamie. After flashing a victorious grin at him, he turned towards the front door. If anything, Adrian was definitely way too sure of himself.

Once outside, Jamie reached out, grabbing a handful of Adrian's ass. "So sexy," he drawled, "that streak of young pride. You gonna live up to it?" Walking alongside Adrian, he leaned to the side, whispering softly. "Gonna fuck me like you mean it, pretty boy?"

An arrogant smirk slide over Adrian's lips as his hand slid behind Jamie, one finger trailing up the center seam of his jeans. "Until you can't stand, lover."

Jamie purred, pale green eyes going dark as they reached the truck. "I can take anything you give me." He licked Adrian's ear, then turned around to unlock the door.

Adrian felt thankful it would be a quick drive home. Trying not to show how much Jamie was getting to him was hard to do. His jeans were already too damn tight as it was. When he slid into the seat, he attempted to readjust the fabric. "It's going to be a long night for you, Jamie. I can promise you that."

Chuckling as he started the truck, Jamie said, "I'm counting on it."

With the low amount of traffic, the drive home went fast. It helped he was in somewhat of a hurry to get back to the apartment. Nothing was said between them, but the rubbing friction of Adrian's hand against Jamie's leg kept both of their minds firmly in the gutter.

Pulling into his parking space, Jamie wasted no time in turning off the truck and getting out. He only waited long enough for Adrian to join him before turning and starting up the stairwell.

Adrian enjoyed the more hurried manner evident in Jamie. Obviously his lover badly wanted him in bed. That was a hell of a rush, and he shared the feeling as well. Adrian wasn't sure how long it would all last, but he was more than eager to go along for the ride for as long as it did.

Slowly unbuttoning his shirt, he followed behind Jamie. When they entered the apartment, he slid off the shirt and dropped it to the floor.

As soon as the door was closed, Jamie tossed his keys onto the bar and locked the door. Pushing Adrian up against the front door, he dropped to his knees, kneading Adrian's cock through his jeans as he worked them open.

"Want to taste you," he said, looking up into Adrian's eyes. "Want that sweet cock sliding over my tongue."

"I thought the cowboy wanted to be ridden hard and long tonight." A lingering gaze roamed over Jamie before Adrian raised his eyes back to the cowboy's face. "Now I'm thinking more of fucking that mouth of yours and then your ass."

One hand unfastened his pants as the other moved to Jamie's hair, fingers tangling tightly in the strands as Adrian's hips nudged persistently towards him. "Open that fucking hot mouth of yours now."

As Adrian's cock sprang free, Jamie purred, "Yes." His tongue slipped out to lick at the tip, tasting the sweet drops. "So good..." He tugged Adrian's jeans further down, fingers cupping Adrian's balls as he opened his mouth, letting Adrian's prick slide over his tongue. He hummed around the hard, hot flesh in his mouth, slowly swallowing more of Adrian's cock.

"Shit." An exhaled hiss drew out the one sound in reaction to the vibration surrounding Adrian. Lazy thrusts of his hips buried his cock repeatedly into the wet depth. He loved the fascinating sight of watching himself disappear over and over again into Jamie's mouth. It distinctly increased his enjoyment and added to the tightening through his groin.

His hand slipped down from Jamie's hair to the side of his face, and a finger traced gently at the corner of his lips. There was something inherently beautiful about having Jamie on his knees in front of him like this. "Fuck. Your mouth feels so fucking good, Jamie. So fucking good."

Jamie hummed again, the sound low and wanton, vibrating up the length of Adrian's cock. His other hand dropped to the front of his pants, pressing the heel of his palm along the hard length of his own cock before he started working his jeans open. In his other hand, he rolled Adrian's balls, tugging and squeezing gently. He worked the flesh in his mouth, tongue sliding along the sensitive underside, giving the head sucking kisses with every pull out. Once his jeans were open, he was able to breathe again. Jamie moved both hands to Adrian's hips, curling his fingers tight, encouraging Adrian to fuck his mouth.

The jerk of Adrian's hips became quicker and harder. He knew it wouldn't take him long at all with the expert manipulation of Jamie's mouth and tongue working him.

"Jamie." A low groan rose in sound as he

suddenly buried himself as deeply as he could in Jamie's mouth. Liquid spilled over Jamie's tongue as Adrian's body shuddered in orgasm.

He hadn't wanted to pull out at the crucial moment, though he probably should have. The blowjob only took the immediate edge off from Adrian. Now he was in the mood to seriously play with the cowboy.

When Adrian's breathing evened out, his hand moved to Jamie's shoulder, drawing him up. The other cupped against Jamie's cock as his lips silenced any words. Adrian tasted himself in the kiss, and he wanted to savor the flavor.

Jamie poured soft, desperate sounds into Adrian's mouth, hips rocking, sliding his cock against Adrian's palm. He buried his fingers in Adrian's hair, tilting Adrian's head just so to deepen the kiss.

Adrian's fingers curled into a tightening slide over Jamie's cock, his other hand reached around and began kneading the cheeks of his ass. As Adrian hungrily devoured his mouth, his thumb rubbed slowly beneath the sensitive underside of his cock just beneath the head.

The movements of Jamie's hips became sharp and quick, gasps pushing into Adrian's mouth with every stroke of Adrian's thumb over Jamie's cock. Fingers tightening on Adrian's head, Jamie cried out into their kiss, hips snapping forward as he came.

Intent on his lover's pleasure, the stroke of Adrian's hand milked Jamie's cock as his mouth took the air from Jamie's. Feeling the trembling of his body, Adrian gentled the kiss to slow brushes of his tongue circling around the cowboy's before releasing him.

"Holy shit," Jamie murmured. "That was...damn." He was reluctant to move, but he was still wanting, still needing to feel Adrian inside him. Pulling away from the kiss, he lifted Adrian's hand to his lips, sucking each finger as he cleaned his come from Adrian's hand. "Bed."

"We both want a hell of a lot more." Chuckling, the sound faded as he watched Jamie cleaning his hand. The tone of his voice altered into a deeper tone. "Now get into the fucking bed, Jamie."

"Mm. Yeah. Bed." Keeping a tight grip on Adrian's hand, Jamie toed off his boots, and stepped out of his jeans. He waited until Adrian had done the same, then he pulled Adrian back to the bedroom. By the time he turned around, his shirt was open and he let go of Adrian's hand to shrug it off. Then he stretched out on the bed, tossing his hat onto the dresser. He pulled up one leg, then let it fall to the side, spreading him open. "See somethin' you want?"

One look at Jamie laying on the bed, his ass open to him, and Adrian's cock started to get hard again. He headed straight for the dresser to get the condom and lube out of the drawer.

"I see something I need to fuck, cowboy." A heavily tinged growl of sound rose in his voice as he moved to the bed.

Grinning like the cat that got the cream, Jamie rested his head back on one arm, the other hand dropping to stroke slowly over his awakening cock. "Want that sweet prick," he said, the Texas drawl thick and low. "Need you to fill me, fuck me through the mattress, Adrian. Hard. Long. Deep." Each word was punctuated by a gasp, and Jamie's thumb pressing into the slit at the tip of his cock with every upstroke.

Only taking the time to open the condom wrapper, Adrian quickly unrolled over the sheath over himself. As he slid over Jamie, his hand knocked Jamie's away before he opened the bottle and coated the rubber with the slippery substance. Once he had the rubber covered, he guided himself, sliding the end of his cock between the crack of Jamie's ass.

"Mm..." Jamie hummed and stretched, arms draping over Adrian's shoulders, fingers sliding through Adrian's hair. "Yeah. C'mon," he urged, hips surging up, legs parting more. "Stop teasin', pretty boy. Push that sweet as fuck cock in and let this cowboy ride."

Adrian's cock nudged slowly into him, dragging out the moment. His hand came up to slide the palm over Jamie's chest before his fingers pinched hard at his left nipple. "C'mon, cowboy, I wanna hear how bad you want it."

Smirking down at him, his tongue darted out to flick over the cowboy's lips as he murmured, "Let me hear you beg for me."

The pinch to his nipple pulled a shout out of Jamie, his body jerking beneath Adrian. "Fuck! Again." One hand left Adrian's hair to cover his hand over Jamie's nipple. "Do it again," he pleaded, chest pushing up as his hips rocked down, driving Adrian's cock deeper. "Oh. Oh, fuck."

The tone of Jamie's voice and the words got to

Adrian. With a sudden hard push, he buried himself fully inside him. Feeling the tightness around him sent a slow shudder through Adrian as his fingers twisted sharply at Adrian's nipple. Lowering his head to Jamie's throat, his teeth closed around his flesh in a sharp bite, stifling the gasp of sound in his own throat.

"Shit!" Jamie jerked, shuddered, breath rushing out of him as every single sensation hit him at once. Wrapping his legs tight around Adrian's waist, he tugged Adrian close, rocking, riding that sweet prick. "Oh, fuck. Fuck yes, Adrian," he groaned. "So fucking good."

Adrian's breath came in ragged gasps in reaction to the grinding rock of Jamie's body. Unable to control the need of his own body, each thrust of his hips drove hard into Jamie's ass. His hand lowered to Jamie's hip, holding him tightly as he fucked him. The overwhelming urge overrode everything else. He wanted his lover over the edge and to hear every moment of it.

Jamie's hand slid between them, curling around his cock. "Fuck. Oh fuck, oh fuck. Don't stop," he panted. "Adrian..." Jamie's eyes flew open, glazed look locking onto Adrian's. He bucked and rocked, fucking himself on Adrian's cock, meeting every thrust Adrian made. After several quick strokes over his cock, Jamie went completely still for the briefest moment before he came, hips rolling as Adrian's name became a desperate chant, heat spilling between them.

Staring down at him, Adrian drank in the sight and sound of his lover getting off. When Jamie cried out to him, the movement of Adrian's hips took on a near bruising pattern before his own body became rigid.

"Jamie, gonna come. Jamie." His nails dig into Jamie's hip as undecipherable sounds escaped him with his release.

Jamie rode out the last tremors of Adrian's orgasm, stroking one hand down Adrian's back, soothing the muscles. "Damn. Just...damn." He breathed easy, eyes closing as the tension ebbed from both of them. "So fine," he whispered, lips teasing over Adrian's cheek. "So fucking fine."

Adrian had never had a lover as vocal and responsive as Jamie. As his body began to relax under Jamie's hand, his eyes ran over Jamie's face. "Fuck, I think listening to you is half the kick, cowboy."

The laugh Jamie gave him sounded low and easy, coming from deep within. "Always been loud," he said, "but with you?" He shook his head and stretched under Adrian. "With you, just can't fucking help it. Wanna let you know how fucking good it feels."

Slowly, Adrian pulled out of Jamie's body before he rolled to his back and sat up. Carefully peeling off the rubber, he tossed it into the trash. Using the sheet, he wiped off the remaining mess. "Feeling you, I tend to lose it."

Adrian laughed but it was more at himself. Sometimes he did feel like he was back in his teens in his own eagerness to fuck the cowboy.

"Mm, I can relate." Jamie stretched and sat up slowly, turning Adrian's head for a slow, soft kiss.

"Shower. Need another shower. Wanna join me?"

"This time I think I will." Still chuckling, he ran his hand slowly over Adrian's chest as he kissed him back. Pulling away, he scooted to the edge of the bed, "Keep doing that and you'll have me horny again."

Laughing, Adrian swatted at his ass as they stood and headed for the bathroom.

PART FOUR

As Jamie slept, Adrian scooted to the edge of the bed. Turning on the small table lamp, he grabbed his pants and dug the vial out of the back pocket. When he dumped the stone in his hand, the sparkling wink of the diamond played in the low light. Only the vibrant pink coloring gave a hint of its true value. A rare pink diamond, and damn near priceless.

Though Adrian could admire the stone for its beauty, he didn't feel the lust to possess Eric had. Adrian far preferred a piece of pink tourmaline over this hunk of stone. But then his personal tastes ran to the more aesthetic than a piece's monetary value.

The irony of a thief preferring tourmaline over a pink diamond struck him. He'd be the first to admit he was an odd bird at this game.

"So what exactly are you doing with a rock like that?" A rather sleepy-looking Jamie stared over at Adrian.

Startled out of his reverie by Jamie's voice, he looked back over his shoulder at him. "I acquired it for Eric. A rock this size and this color is hard to come by. Normally pink diamonds of less than a carat aren't too hard to get. But anything over a carat, and you're talking close to a million. This little baby is three carats."

An eyebrow rose at that. "*Acquired* it? Should I be expecting cops at my door anytime soon?"

Giving Jamie a guarded look, Adrian added,

"No, why?"

Jamie sat up and slid back until he was leaning against the headboard of the bed, letting the sheet fall to his lap. "Unless you're a broker or a jeweler, it takes a good bit of—style—for someone to gain possession of something like that."

A faint smirk curled his lips. "You could call me a broker. I negotiate for things when Eric doesn't want his name brought into it."

Adrian left it unsaid that it also included when somebody didn't want to go along with whatever Eric wanted.

"Uh-huh." A slow smile crawled across Jamie's lips. "You're a thief."

Adrian turned to face Jamie and met his gaze steadily.

"Interesting line of work." Jamie winked at him as he grinned.

Silently, Adrian slipped the diamond back into the vial, then slid it back into the pocket. A slight relaxation in his frame became apparent with Jamie's comment. Though he wouldn't say a damn thing.

Jamie nodded. "So long as you don't bring cops to my door or the shop, I'm not gonna question it. I trust you."

"Not something I can promise." There were no real guarantees in his line of work. He didn't live his life like he was going to end up in jail, but the prospect was there. "But the less I say, the better off you are."

"Well, with that answer, at least I know you'll try." He got out of the bed and stretched. "And I gotta thank you for your honesty, and for not bolting when I guessed what you are."

This wasn't a situation Adrian had ever been in. The people he slept with didn't get roped into helping him find something he'd lost, nor did they even know he was a thief. "If anything ever happens, as far as I'm concerned you don't know a damn thing. And you don't know a damn thing either if anybody asks."

Watching him stretch, Adrian smiled. "Running would be rather stupid. Like locking the barn after the horse bolted."

"I know nothin'," Jamie said, winking at him. "Not a damn thing." He bent over and started rummaging through the dresser, looking for a pair of shorts. "Want some coffee?"

"Yeah, I could use a cup." Adrian felt the stirring as his cock hardened at the sight of Jamie bent over, leaving the delectable ass exposed to his view. Grabbing for his jeans, he quickly slipped them on before standing up. "I promised Gerald I'd meet him at the beach sometime this morning."

"Gerald?" Jamie asked as he slipped on a pair of sinfully-short blue jean cutoffs.

"An old friend of mine." Adrian shrugged as he slipped on his shirt. "He's got a house on the beach. And I usually drop by there on Fridays."

"Ah."

After putting his shoes on, he followed Jamie out into the kitchen. "I also need to put this damn rock in a safe place."

At the moment, Adrian had a few other things on his mind and kept any wayward thoughts about Jamie severely under wraps.

"Thought it was for DeSalvo?" Jamie asked as he started the coffee. "Why don't you just take it to him?"

"Because Eric is out of town until Tuesday. So I need to hold onto it for a few more." Eyeing him, he asked, "Wanna come with? We can go to Gerald's. It's worth a couple of beers and a nice swim."

Catching his bottom lip in his teeth for a moment, Jamie finally nodded. "Yeah, sure. I'd like that. I need to take anything? Beer? Snacks? Rubbers? Lube?

"Nah, Gerald's well supplied. He just requires bodies." When the coffee was done, Adrian helped himself to a cup.

"Oh." Jamie jumped up onto the counter and leaned back, legs spread as he shifted to get comfortable. "Body. Yeah. I can do that," he muttered absently as he sipped his coffee.

Giving him an odd look, Adrian said, "You'll see what I mean when we get there, and it's not what I think you're thinking. If that's what you're thinking."

"Good Lord. Am I that obvious?"

"It was the 'I can do that'. I figured you might be thinking orgy or something." Laughing heartily, he took a sip of the hot coffee and ended up burning his lip. "Oww. Fuck."

Jamie chuckled and sipped his coffee slowly. "If you weren't in a hurry, I'd know what cures that."

Adrian grinned. "I'm not the most graceful when I first wake up. Why don't you go ahead and get dressed. You can drive us over to Gerald's whenever you're ready."

Finishing off his coffee, Jamie jumped off the

counter and put the mug in the sink. As he walked by Adrian, he leaned close to whisper in his ear. "Don't have to be graceful to get your cock sucked." Then he continued on to the bedroom, whistling 'Rodeo' by Garth Brooks.

As determined as Adrian seemed to be not to get sidetracked by Jamie, Jamie seemed intent on distracting him. Ignoring the twinge in his nether regions, he sipped his coffee as he waited for Jamie to return.

A few minutes later, Jamie came in, tight jeans hugging his ass as he bent over to put his boots on. When he stood back up, he turned and caught Adrian in a coffee-flavored kiss, tongue pushing into Adrian's mouth. This was one thing he was determined to get.

Okay, Adrian could be sidetracked a little. The scrape of his teeth ran along Jamie's tongue as his body shifted closer to him. One hand slipped up into Jamie's hair as Adrian nibbled lightly at him.

Jamie moaned softly, tongue fucking Adrian's lips like he really wanted to do to the man's ass. But that would have to wait. Still, he couldn't help but slide his hands down to cup said ass.

Finally, Adrian managed to pull away from him, muttering, "We better get going."

Grumbling, Jamie nodded. "Yeah. Otherwise I'm likely to drop to my knees or bend you over the fucking table." He grabbed his keys and wallet, then looked back at Adrian.

Not addressing his comments, Adrian moved for the door.

After dropping off the diamond at his house, it

didn't take more than five minutes to get to Gerald's. The small, squat house was oddly run down in such a pricey neighborhood. Parking in the driveway, Jamie turned off the truck. As Adrian got out, he waved at the old man standing on the porch.

"Bout time your ass got here, Adrian."

Jamie hung back for a minute, waiting until they'd said their hellos before tipping his hat to Gerald. "Mornin'. Name's Jamie Holland. It's a pleasure."

Gerald grinned and held out a hand. "Gerald Maxwell. Nice to meet you."

Adrian watched as they shook hands. "Make sure you count your fingers, Jamie. Just in case they all aren't there anymore."

Grinning at the voodoo priest, he said, "I figured you wouldn't mind me dragging Jamie along, Gerald. We're both in the mood for a couple of cold beers and a swim. How's business been?"

Jamie blinked and Gerald just laughed.

"Eh, it's been. Come on in, guys." Gerald waved them into the house.

Opening the wooden screen door, Adrian stepped over the dog stretched out in front of the doorway.

"Aunt Agga, move your old ass so we can get through." At Gerald's command, the dog slowly got up and wandered out the door to sleep on the porch.

Following them in, Gerald passed Adrian to go into the kitchen. When he returned he had three bottles of Budweiser in hand. After he passed them out, Adrian walked through the house and out to the back porch. Picking one of the old chairs, he sat down and opened the beer. "Damn, I really should get out here more often, Gerald."

The sound of the wash of the shore on the sand reached them from over Gerald's backyard sand dune. The water's edge wasn't more than thirty feet away.

"Wow," Jamie said as he sat down beside Adrian, beer in hand. "Been a long time since I've been to the beach."

He let his head fall back and his eyes close as he just listened to the waves. Before long, the bottle was nestled between his legs as Jamie dozed off.

In companionable silence, Adrian and Gerald drank their beers. When the sound of Jamie's deepening breathing reached him, Gerald looked over at Adrian. "So how long has this one been around?"

Shrugging, Adrian gazed out at the small strip of ocean visible from the porch. "A few days."

"He don't seem like no bottom to me, boy. Big strapping fellow like that. He's gonna like his cock dipped, too."

Adrian just shrugged.

Gerald raised an eyebrow. "So he's not a keeper?" He'd known Adrian for well over half the man's life; a fool Gerald wasn't. He could read the signals Jamie was giving off, but he figured Adrian would learn them sooner or later.

"Have I ever had a keeper?" Giving him a mild look, Adrian took a taste of his beer before he added, "And no, I don't need no charms, Gerald."

Gerald snorted. "For this one? You won't need 'em, kid."

Adrian just gave him a confused look. "You know better than to be settling me down, Gerald. Keep the matchmaking for the rest of your grandkids."

A laugh followed his words, showing he took no offense to the old man's meddling habits.

"If you ain't interested in goin' further, then I ain't the one you need be worryin' about, Adrian." Gerald didn't look at him, just looked out over the ocean as he drank his beer. "He likes you. A lot. Can see it in his eyes."

"After a few days?" Adrian didn't mean to scoff, but it was hard to imagine Jamie cared one way or the other about him. Love at first sight was only in romance novels.

Gerald shrugged. "Happened with me an' my Laura. Blessed her sweet heart; I fell in love the first time I saw 'er." He turned a shrewd, but loving gaze, on Adrian. "Don't lead him on. If you plan on keepin' him out of your heart, you'd best be breakin' things off soon. I got the notion you're wormin' your way into his, though he's not likely to tell you."

Adrian had no clue what to say to Gerald's comments. Glancing over at Jamie's sleeping form, he frowned slightly before he murmured, "You know there's no place for complications in my life, Gerald. It's enough of a mess already."

Leaning slightly towards Adrian, Gerald whispered. "Love don't have to be a complication. If you don't want him, let him go—before someone gets hurt."

Finishing off his beer, Adrian didn't say anything to him. Finally he just nodded before he tossed the empty bottle into a nearby trash can. "Got another beer? I think I need it."

"In the fridge. Grab me another while you're up."

Pushing from the chair, Adrian ambled back into the house. Gerald was a notorious packrat. Piles of papers and boxes cluttered the majority of the house into small pathways. Digging in the fridge, he grabbed a couple more beers before returning to the porch. "Gerald, when you gonna let me get a cleaning crew in here?"

Adrian really didn't want to continue their earlier discussion so instead he choose to tease the old man. Just as he always did. Handing him the beer, he settled back into the chair.

"When I'm dead an' gone." Gerald nodded his thanks as he opened the bottle. "So what's that ass gotten you into now?"

"Dead and gone. Yeah, right." Rolling his eyes, he opened his own beer. "Which ass are you referring to?"

With a wink, he lifted his bottle, toasting Gerald before he took a drink.

Gerald chuckled, the aged sound rich and deep. "I know what your ass has gotten you into. Was talkin' about DeSalvo."

Glancing over at the sleeping Jamie, Adrian had to chuckle. "Ole da, if only you knew."

Forcing his thoughts from that pleasing occupation, he looked back at Gerald. "Since I'm getting a hundred thou from him this time, I ain't got no complaints."

Pausing to give him a severe look, Adrian added, "No cursing my employer either. It's my only source of cash right now."

Feigning offense, Gerald gasped. "Me? Never. Da Master takes care of my Adrian," he drawled in a thick, if not wholly genuine, Southern accent. "He'd just best be keepin' those paws from you. I don't think your Jamie would take kindly to it."

Leveling a bland, disbelieving look on Gerald, Adrian muttered, "Umm, yeah. Master, my ass. Eric never keeps his hands to himself. An annoyance but as long as he doesn't push it, I'm fine. So you can keep your curses for more deserving people."

Pausing again, he eyed the old man before he continued, "And he's not *my* Jamie."

"Won't argue with you no more on either account," Gerald conceded. "But mark my words, Adrian, someone is goin' to get hurt if you aren't mindful." He took a long drink of beer before adding, "I love you. You know that. You know that's why I'm tellin' you this shit now."

Resorting to his own beer, he hastily chugged a good portion of it down. "Dammit, Gerald, I know. You've got to be wrong on him though. It's a piece of ass, nothing more. To me and to him."

He deliberately kept his voice low, not wanting to wake up Jamie with this conversation. Glancing over at the cowboy, Adrian couldn't help the lingering gaze as it traveled slowly over the sleeping body. Damn, but Jamie was fucking hot. In bed and out of bed. To have to give that up and so soon just didn't seem fair.

Gerald huffed just as Jamie began to stir.

"Oh. Damn. Sorry. Didn't mean to doze like that," Jamie muttered sleepily. Looking over at

Adrian, he gave him a quick wink. "Was up late. I miss anything?"

"Only the chance at a second beer, cowboy." Grinning, he hoisted his bottle and finished it off. He hadn't missed the disgruntled sound from Gerald and didn't dare risk a side glance at him. Instead Adrian set the empty bottle down.

"Damn." Jamie grimaced as he held up his bottle. "Must've been out a bit; beer's gone warm." Still, he tipped it up and drained well over half the nearly-full beer in one lengthy swallow.

"Why don't you two take a swim? I got some business that needs tending to. There's more beer in the fridge, so just help yourselves." Gerald stood and gathered up the empty bottles. After directing a severe look at Adrian, he turned towards Jamie. "Nobody'll bother you two on the beach. They wouldn't dare."

Adrian managed to look everywhere but at Gerald. Still he could feel the weight of the stare before it passed him by.

"Swim in the ocean? Sounds damn fine to me." Jamie looked over at Adrian, licking at his lips as his grin widened. "You up for it, pretty boy?"

"One of the reasons I came out here, Jamie." Leaning forward in his chair, he pulled his shirt over his head.

Giving the back door a quick glance, Jamie took off his shirt, then stood and walked over to Adrian, holding out a hand for him. "Now that's a sight I could look at for a long time. Comin'?"

Adrian had enjoyed the secluded beach for most of his life. He'd spend hours exploring the small coves in his early teen years. Taking Jamie's hand, he maneuvered out of the chair as he unfastened his own pants. "How long has it been since you went skinny dipping, cowboy?"

"Too long," Jamie murmured, voice gone husky as he brushed Adrian's hands away, taking over the task of undressing Adrian. He pushed Adrian's pants to the ground and looked down, licking his lips. "Wish I could swallow you down right now," he whispered, fingertips just barely tracing down the shaft of Adrian's cock.

Instantly Adrian's mind became clouded with the surge of need sweeping through him. He groaned as his hand caught at Jamie's. With so little effort, Adrian was already hard and his hand pressed the cowboy's against himself.

"Swim first." Biting at his lower lip, he attempted to clear the hazing of his thoughts. As he stared into Jamie's eyes, he tried to read him.

"Yeah, pretty boy. Swim first." Giving Adrian's cock a light squeeze, Jamie leaned close enough for a teasing kiss before pulling away to finish undressing. He gave Adrian a wink and turned, heading out onto the sand of the private patch of beach.

Fuck, it seemed like Jamie had him in the palm of his hand, and in more ways than one. Standing where he'd been left, Adrian's eyes followed him as he walked over the dune. Gerald had to be wrong. His grandfather had to be fucking wrong.

In warning, the twinge throbbing though his cock made him follow behind Jamie. Almost tripping over his own pants, he had to kick out to get the material off of his leg. It was just sex, and that was all.

"Come on, pretty boy," Jamie called in an almost-sing song way, splashing into the crashing waves. "Sweet Jesus, that's cold!"

Finally Adrian barreled after him. He hit the surf right after Jamie and very quickly waded out until he could dive into the water. It wouldn't take long for the initial chill to warm up. The day was a hot one and the water felt good against his heated skin. He even welcomed the harsh wake up to his groin.

A few moments later, Jamie emerged from under a wave, light brown hair slicked back, reaching a little past his shoulders. He watched Adrian swim, loved the way the sun caught across the muscled body sparkling with sea water. Then he closed his eyes to the sight. And he purposely ignored the tiny ache in his chest.

Seeming completely at home in the water, Adrian deliberately dove deeper into the water as he turned in Jamie's direction. He emerged a few seconds later, not too far off from the cowboy. Clearly, he loved the ocean and swimming.

Jamie closed the distance between them, reaching out for Adrian. Taking hold of one of Adrian's wrists, he pulled Adrian close, bringing him in for a kiss. He didn't care where they were. Here, with the ocean waves crashing around them and Adrian's lips on his, he was in sheer Heaven.

Adrian's lips slowly brushed over Jamie's, coaxing a response from him. As he slid his arms around the cowboy's neck, his body leaned in against him.

"Want you," Jamie mouthed against Adrian's

slick skin, the kisses raining down over Adrian's throat. Jamie licked the salt water away, body near burning as he slid both hands around to cup Adrian's ass, pulling them together, rubbing their cocks alongside each other. "Need you, Adrian."

The tighter press of their bodies trapped their cocks against each other. Another groan escaped Adrian as his hands slid into Jamie's hair. "Need you too, Jamie. So badly."

Jamie nodded, mouth still sliding over Adrian's throat, licking the water from every inch of skin he could reach. He started backing up, pulling Adrian with him, until they hit dry land. Then he hooked one leg over Adrian's hip and they tumbled to the sand, the waves sliding up under them as he rocked into Adrian's body, grabbing onto Adrian's ass to pull him down harder.

"I'm clean," he murmured, lips moving back up to Adrian's mouth. You're the first in several years. Please tell me you're clean."

Adrian ended up landing on top of him, his body grinding more tightly into him. Drawing his head back, he stared down at Jamie. "I'm clean, but neither of us needs to take the chance."

How he managed to even rationalize in the situation was beyond both of them. Sliding downward, his lips pressed a trail of kisses and light nips of teeth over Jamie's skin. Nestling between Jamie's legs, he lowered his head. The flick of his tongue traveled the length of his cock before his mouth took him in.

"Fuck!" Jamie's eyes went wide and his hips snapped up, the sensation of Adrian's lips drowning out everything else. His fingers slid through Adrian's hair, not directing, just holding, petting. "Oh, God. Your mouth. So sweet." He was babbling, hips rolling beneath Adrian, cock pushing between those sweet fucking lips.

The brush of his hand caressed over Jamie's balls before sliding beneath them. Applying a light circular pressure to the skin underneath, he let Jamie fuck his mouth. The rapid glide of tongue and teeth taking him deeply before the suction of his mouth let him go.

"Adrian. Fuck. Gonna come..." Jamie panted, holding Adrian's head as he started to thrust into his mouth. The velvet heat of Adrian's mouth set him on fire, scorching every inch of Jamie's flesh until he was sure he would turn to ashes.

His free hand moved to Jamie's chest, and his fingers lightly pinched at the already hard nipple. The pressure of his mouth kept a tight suction on Jamie's cock, He took each of the harder thrusts of Jamie's hips, pulling him as deeply into his mouth as he could. The flat of his tongue added another enticing sensation, bent on sending Jamie right over the edge.

Jamie's breath left him in a rush and he shouted Adrian's name, cock throbbing hard in Adrian's mouth. Trapped between Adrian's mouth and those fingers tweaking his nipple, Jamie could only ride it out, writhing on the sand. When the last of the aftershocks began to fade, he sucked in several deep breaths, fingers easing on Adrian's head.

"Holy fuck. Sweet Jesus, that was fucking good."

Swallowing the salty sweetness, he cleaned

Jamie off before he lifted his head. Smiling rakishly, he said, "I aim to please, cowboy."

Oddly, the act of giving had taken off the worst edge of his own need. Adrian basked in the response Jamie had given him and in the expression on his face.

"C'mere." Jamie tugged Adrian up his body and took a kiss, tongue swiping over Adrian's lips. He reached down and curled his fingers around Adrian's cock, tugging slow and easy. "What's your pleasure, pretty boy?"

His mental answer to Jamie's question nearly shocked Adrian. For the moment, he simply needed to be with Jamie. The torturous teasing of his fingers scattered any kind of thought before he could focus clearly on it. Now he wanted to fuck Jamie in the worst possible way. At this point, he didn't even care if Jamie fucked him. Everything this man did felt good. Raising his head, he stared down at him, murmuring in a husky voice, "You need to take me home. Right now."

A heated glaze filmed over his eyes as the tightening worsened in his body. "Please, fucking take me home. I need you too damn badly."

"Done and done," Jamie growled. He kissed Adrian hard and scrambled out from under him and onto his feet. Taking Adrian's hand in his, he led the way back to the house. Surprising even himself, he dressed in record time.

Adrian dressed just as quickly though it was obvious from the tightness of his pants, he had one hell of a problem. Something that wouldn't be satisfied by anything less than them fucking. As they moved back through Gerald's house, he called out to his grandfather, "See you next Friday, ole da."

The sound of Gerald's grunt answered him from the direction of the bedroom as Adrian pulled Jamie with him out the front door and towards the truck.

The ride home was tense and quiet, and they both could practically feel the need buzzing between them. As soon as the car was off, Jamie got out and waited for Adrian, near bouncing with need.

Brushing past Jamie, Adrian headed into the building. When they were inside Jamie's apartment, Adrian shut the door and turned to look at him. He didn't care what Jamie did to him, and it clearly showed in his eyes.

Standing there, staring at him, Adrian couldn't move. Shakily, his hand reached out for Jamie.

Jamie pulled Adrian to him, his cock already hardening again. Soon as the door was closed, he shoved Adrian against it, crushing their mouths together, tongue pushing between Adrian's lips. He worked Adrian's pants open, then his own, shoving them to the floor until their cocks pressed tightly together. He gasped into Adrian's mouth, hips grinding.

"Want inside you. Please, Adrian."

The friction between them was an exquisite, continuous torture to Adrian. He clung to Jamie, letting himself go to it. When he could answer Jamie, the words came from him in gasps of breath. "Anything. Just fuck me."

"Bed." Jamie moved into the bedroom, heading for the bedside table. He got a rubber out and the bottle of lube, setting them on the table. "Want inside that sweet body," he said, smiling as he pulled Adrian close, easing him down onto the bed.

Desperate for the sensation that would release him and give him what he wanted, Adrian would do about anything Jamie told him to. His arms and legs tangled with Jamie's as they stretched out on the bed. "I want you inside me, Jamie."

Before he could say more, he lifted his head and caught Jamie's lips with his own. The arch of his body slid against Jamie's as he hungrily kissed him.

"Shh..." Jamie murmured on Adrian's lips. He spread Adrian's legs slowly and settled between them, hands stroking down Adrian's sides, just petting and soothing. "We have all the time in the world. Just relax and feel."

Slipping one hand between Adrian's legs, he kneaded Adrian's balls and pressed a fingertip to the soft skin just behind them.

Adrian felt as if he was on fire and each little touch fanned the flames. A low groan escaped him as he closed his eyes, feeling the manipulation of Jamie's fingers. His hips arched towards his hand unable to still his impatience.

Starting at the hollow of Adrian's throat, Jamie worked his way down Adrian's body, kisses followed by nips of his teeth, his tongue soothing away the burn. Moving over Adrian's chest, he closed his mouth over one of Adrian's nipples, worrying it with his teeth, then stroking his tongue over the aching flesh. His finger slid lower to circle Adrian's hole, just enough to tease. When he closed his lips around Adrian's nipple and began sucking on it, Jamie pressed his fingertip to Adrian's ass, adding a bit of pressure without penetration.

"You're fucking driving me crazy, Jamie." His hands slide up to Jamie's hair, letting his fingers run slowly through the strands. The light pressure was enough to make Adrian's body jerk slightly. The need rippled through him, heightening with Jamie's teasing. He wanted more than anything to be fucked by him.

"Mmm," Jamie hummed, sliding down Adrian's body. Then he pushed Adrian's legs up and apart, bending to lick the soft sac, sucking gently on first one ball and then the other. Any attempts on Adrian's part to guide Jamie to his cock failed. He settled lower and looked up at Adrian's face just as he flicked his tongue over Adrian's hole. "Hold your legs for me."

Pure sensation jolted through him with the small flick of that tongue. Letting go of Jamie's head, he grabbed hold of his own thighs as he drew his legs up. He'd nearly forgotten how damn good it could feel to be played with like this.

His hands free to play and touch, Jamie dove in, tongue pushing into Adrian as he spread Adrian open. He moaned softly, immersing himself in this simple act, hands caressing the backs of Adrian's thighs, cupping his balls and tugging them gently. His tongue darted in and out of Adrian's ass, circling the outside before plunging back in, deep and quick.

"Oh. Fuck." His fingers tightened against his legs as his body writhed with the molten fire caused by Jamie's tongue. "Please, Jamie, please."

Adrian needed and wanted a hell of a lot more. One hand tried to reach for his lover, to draw him back up.

Jamie pulled away and reached for the lube and the rubber as he slid back up to kiss Adrian hard. As he fucked Adrian's mouth with his tongue, he rested his hands above Adrian's head long enough to rip open the package. Sitting back on his heels, he sheathed his cock then slicked it up, biting at his lip while staring down at the sight before him. When he leaned back down, he brushed his lips over Adrian's as he slowly pushed two fingers deep inside him.

Groaning in reaction, his hands curled tightly to Jamie's upper arms as his hips tried to push down. Inner muscles tightened around the fingers, drawing another soft sound from Adrian. Every part of him pinpointed to the one lone sensation, and his nails dug slightly into Jamie's skin, holding tightly to him.

Adding a third finger, Jamie opened Adrian up, raining soft kisses over Adrian's face and neck. "Ready for me, baby?"

Unable to form coherent words, Adrian could only nod. It had been so long since he'd let anybody fuck him. Right at the moment, how badly he wanted Jamie was the only thing he could focus on. His entire body tightened with the thought. The fingers were driving his body into a near frenzied state of need as he tried to rock harder on them.

"Easy," Jamie whispered, withdrawing his fingers. He lined himself up and pushed, slow and gentle. As the tight heat of Adrian's body surrounded him, pulling him in, Jamie watched Adrian's eyes, never once looking away. It was then that something inside him melted and sparked all at once.

Staring up at him, Adrian's eyes widened, reflecting the intensity of feeling absorbing him. Sliding his hands up over his arms, they rested against Jamie's back before his fingers caressed over his skin.

He was lost. Jamie was lost and he knew it. Resting his forehead to Adrian's, he slid the rest of the way in, not daring to move, just letting Adrian get used to him being there. He kept himself propped on his left forearm by Adrian's head, while he slid the other hand down Adrian's face, fingers stroking the smooth skin of his cheek. Yeah. He was falling hard, harder than he ever had before.

As Jamie settled inside his body, Adrian's hands ran down to the curve of his ass. A light press kept him where he was. Tipping his face up, he pressed a soft kiss to Jamie's lips as he whispered, "I'd forgotten how damn good this could feel."

Before long Adrian's body started to slowly rock against him. The rest of his words came out in groan. "Fuck me, Jamie. Now. Just fuck me."

Capturing Adrian's mouth in a deep, hungry kiss, Jamie began doing just that. His strokes were long and deep, every push into Adrian's body sending another bolt of pleasure straight up Jamie's spine. Without breaking the kiss, he reached back and grabbed Adrian's hands, pinning them tightly to the bed above Adrian's head as the slow strokes turned to thrusts, Jamie's tongue fucking Adrian's lips in the same maddening rhythm.

The slow movement only served to push Adrian towards the edge without letting him find the release his body craved. Writhing beneath Jamie, his nails rhythmically flexed into Jamie's hands. The deeper thrusts made Adrian's body strain to the one above him. Need coiled with incessant pressure and tightened in quickening pulses through his entire body. The constant rubbing within and the friction of skin over his cock promised so much, but Jamie kept it just beyond his grasp. Near desperate, he tried to slide his own hand free to reach his cock.

Letting go of Adrian's hands, Jamie pushed up on one hand while curling the other around Adrian's cock. Every hard thrust drove him deeper inside Adrian and the rhythm of his hand matched them, fingers tightening as he jerked Adrian off.

"Come on," he urged, need riding the words as he fucked Adrian hard and deep. "Come for me, Adrian."

Jamie had increased the need of Adrian's body to a near fever pitch. Helpless to it, his hips bucked beneath Jamie.

"Ah. Fuck." Adrian managed to get that out before his breath was stolen from him. Shuddering violently, Adrian tumbled into the orgasm as it rushed through his entire body. Its intensity left him suspended until shorter, sharper pulses echoed inside him with the hot spill of come slicking between them.

"Jamie." The sharp cry called to his lover, threaded with the pleasure flooding him. He'd never felt anything so fucking intense in his life. Trying to focus on Jamie, he wanted to see his lover lose it as well. The arch of his body ground tightly to Jamie's in a hard rocking motion.

Jamie's eyes went wide and he ground out

Adrian's name, hips pounding into Adrian. Several hard thrusts sent him over the edge, the pleasure rocketing up his spine, his cock pulsing deep inside Adrian's body as he came. He pushed his tongue into Adrian's mouth, riding the last of his orgasm, biting back the urge to shout the last thing he knew Adrian wanted to hear.

Adrian's body clung to his. A part of the pleasure came from hearing and feeling Jamie lost in his own climax. Jamie definitely qualified as the best fucking lover Adrian had ever had. Adrian could barely move now. The initial harder urgency of their kiss slowly became more leisurely as Adrian's tongue circled Jamie's in flicking caresses.

Jamie seemed in no real hurry to move, nor did he seem inclined to pull out just yet. He brought his hand up and broke from the kiss to lick it clean, winking at Adrian.

"Would it be cliché for me to say that was the best damn sex I've ever had?"

"Just don't fucking move. Not yet." Grinning up at him, Adrian slid his arms around Jamie's neck. "Then I'm as clichéd as you are because I've never felt anything that fucking good. You made me completely lose it."

"Yeah. Same here, pretty boy." The words were whispered on Adrian's lips and Jamie kissed him softly. "Same here."

PART FIVE

It seemed they were living in each other's pockets. Adrian wasn't sure how it got that way, but he couldn't complain. He'd been going to Jamie's shop around four every day before closing time. Afterwards they'd go out to dinner or often as not they ended up going to either Jamie's place or his, and tumbling into bed.

Entering the shop, Adrian quietly closed the door and headed straight to Jamie's work room in the back. Leaning against the door frame, he watched the cowboy bent over his table, intently working.

With the precision of a surgeon, Jamie drew the knife down the glass, following the outline of the angel's wing. Alan Jackson was on the radio, singing about it being five o'clock somewhere. When Jimmy Buffet joined in with Alan, Jamie started singing as well, the Texas drawl coming out full and strong. His hips moved slightly as he shifted his feet, almost dancing. Not once did the knife falter from its path on the glass.

As tempted as he was to just walk up behind Jamie, Adrian resisted because he didn't want to startle his lover while cutting glass. Clearing his throat lightly, he pushed from the door and moved towards him.

Looking up, Jamie grinned. "Hi, pretty boy. Just trying to get this wing cut out. It's part of a piece I'm doing for DeSalvo." He stepped back so Adrian could see the rest. "It's the pivotal scene between Lucifer and the Archangel Michael."

"Am I interrupting your work?" Standing beside him, Adrian looked over the patterns laid on the table. To say Jamie had an impressive skill would be mild. The intricate design of the angel defeating his foe was clearly a masterpiece. At least from Adrian's perspective. Murmuring softly, he added, "I really hope Eric is paying you one hell of a salary on this."

"Oh, yeah. Well over three month's income is coming from this piece alone. Not sure how he found my name, but I'm damn glad he did." Setting the glass cutter down, Jamie tipped his hat back and turned Adrian's head for a kiss. "Mm," he murmured on Adrian's lips. "How was your day, sexy?"

Nipping gently at Jamie's lip, he enjoyed the brief kiss. "Considering my apartment is wall to wall people right now, I came here for some peace and quiet. And he'd better be paying you well. Eric can be a cheap bastard when he thinks he can get away with it. "

"We can always order in," Jamie suggested. "Or we can go out, if you're feeling up to it. Then there's always my place." He placed a soft, chaste kiss on Adrian's lips and gave him a wink before turning to put things away. "So what's up with the crowd at your place?"

"Order in. I'm in the mood to stay in tonight, Jamie." As tired as he was, he didn't really want to go out anywhere. "It's healing day, and everybody in the blasted neighborhood hangs out, waiting for Nostradamus. They'll be gone before we get there. Else I'll throw them all out."

Turning, Adrian leaned carefully against the

table. Folding his arms against his chest, he watched Jamie. Most of the time, his eyes never really strayed from the cowboy. He got way too much enjoyment out of watching the lanky movements of his body. And the view of the fine ass encased in tight denim was guaranteed to keep his eyes where they ought to be.

Jamie opened his mouth as if he was going to say something, but closed it at the last minute. "I'll ask about healing day later," he laughed as he covered the table with a white sheet. Setting his hat back in place, he smiled over at Adrian. "Come on, pretty boy. Let's head home. Chinese or Italian?"

Yes, Adrian led a strange life, and he knew it. Nobody needed to mention anything about it. "Umm, Chinese. Sweet and sour chicken would hit the spot nicely."

Heading towards the front of the shop, Adrian moved in front of Jamie. Keeping his hands stuffed in his pockets kept them off Jamie. "Then maybe a movie or some TV to relax by."

"Movies are good," Jamie said, sounding a bit distracted as he walked behind Adrian. "Damn, you have a sweet ass."

"Food first, then the subject of my ass and yours after." Turning his head to look back at Jamie, Adrian smirked at him. "We'll discuss it during the movie."

When the front door opened, and one of Jamie's customers came in, Adrian paused near the counter, leaning against it to wait.

"Howdy, ma'am," Jamie drawled, slipping his hat off to the woman. "How can I help you?"

"I ordered a piece about two weeks ago," she

said, handing Jamie a slip of paper.

"Oh! Yes, Mrs. Southers. One moment." He disappeared back into the workshop and returned a minute later carrying a small oval wrapped in white cloth. "He's a very pretty subject to work from."

The woman's face lit up like a Christmas tree when she unwrapped the oval to reveal the stained glass portrait of a cocker spaniel. "He's beautiful! Oh, thank you so much."

"Thank you, ma'am. It was a pleasure."

Giving Jamie a smile, she set the oval on the front desk and rummaged through her purse, finally coming out with two twenty dollar bills. "Thanks again."

Jamie took the money and smiled. "Come back anytime, ma'am." He waited until she was out before opening up the safe under the desk. "Just let me get the rest of the day's earnings out. Need to drop by the bank." He stuffed the handful of bills into a bank money bag and closed the safe before standing. "Ready when you are."

Once Jamie was ready, Adrian nodded before walking towards the door. "You do a lot of personalized work?"

"Oh, yeah," Jamie said as he locked the door. "I prefer it, actually." He tilted his head and looked at Adrian for a moment. "You'd look real good in glass."

Moving towards Jamie's truck, he looked over at him. "Is that a hint I should commission you to do a piece?"

Chuckling, Adrian opened the passenger door and slid in.

"I'll cut you a deal, pretty boy. Half now and half

when it's done." Jamie gave him a wicked grin as he started the truck, making it very clear that money had nothing to do with payment.

"And do I get a personal, hands-on inspection of the subject you're going to create in glass?" Smirking slightly, he eyed Jamie as he fastened the seatbelt.

Jamie licked his lips as he backed out of the parking space. Tossing a wink Adrian's way, he said, "I think I'll do a portrait of you jerking off. Keep it in my bedroom — for when I'm needin', and you're not there."

Adrian burst out laughing. "You'll never have your mind out of the gutter. But you know, I'd let you. As long as you kept it for your private enjoyment."

"I'm with you," Jamie shot back. "Not like I can even attempt to keep my mind out of the gutter. You're sex on legs, Adrian."

Adrian gave him a smug look as if to say *I know*. "All right, I commission you to make a stain glass piece of me jerking off. Now where we getting the food from?"

"There's a great Chinese place a block from the bank. You'll love it." Giving Adrian a wink, Jamie started the truck and backed out. He turned down the radio to keep from blowing Adrian out of the cab with Garth Brooks, and a few minutes later, he pulled into the bank parking lot.

"I'll be right back." He leaned over and gave Adrian a kiss before sliding out of the truck and making his way towards the front door.

After Jamie got out of the truck, Adrian quickly turned off the radio station. A few minutes later, he turned it back on and tried to find a better station. The sound of Disturbed filled the truck and he settled back to wait patiently for Jamie to return.

When Jamie opened the door, he grimaced as he got in. "Can't handle Garth, huh? Gotta admit: David Draiman looks much better."

Giving him a side look, a brow rose slightly as Adrian said, "If you know who he is, you should listen to him more often."

Laughing, Jamie pulled back out onto the street. "I do sometimes. It's just that I was born and raised in Texas. Country music is in my blood." When they got to the restaurant, he looked over at Adrian. "Want to come in and order? Or do you trust me?"

"We need to thin your blood a bit." Laughing, Adrian opened the truck door and got out. "I trust you, but I'm coming along anyway."

He followed behind Jamie into the restaurant. Admiring the view as they walked, he whistled an off tune, innocent sounding little piece.

Jamie slipped off his hat and looked through the menu spread out under the glass on the counter. "What looks good to you, pretty boy?"

"Sweet and sour chicken, some fried rice, and an extra of teriyaki beef. Don't forget the fortune cookies." Grinning at Jamie, Adrian didn't even look at the menu. He already knew what he wanted.

"Sounds good." Jamie looked up and smiled at the man behind the counter. "Make that two, double what he said."

The man rang up their food, took the money, and a few minutes later thanked them as he handed Jamie the food. Setting his hat back on his head,

Jamie grabbed the bags and led the way out.

As they left the restaurant, Adrian couldn't resist speeding up his steps enough to cup his hand over Jamie's ass. In a low voice, he murmured, "Fuck. Can't wait to get that ass home."

With another grin, he slipped around to the passenger side of the truck and got in.

The second they both were in the truck, Jamie set the bags on the bench seat between them and leaned over. Grabbing Adrian's chin, he pulled him in for a deep, heated kiss. "Want that sweet cock," he murmured on Adrian's lips before pulling away.

When Adrian finally caught a breath after that kiss, he chuckled, "You play hard ball, Jamie."

Reaching over nonchalantly, he rested his hand on Jamie's thigh, lightly scratching his nails against the denim.

Jamie groaned and slid just a bit lower in the seat, effectively pushing Adrian's hand over his cock as he started the truck. "Oh, I can assure you. What's hard under there ain't a ball."

Idly, Adrian's fingers brushed back and forth across the material. A grin came out when he felt the hard outline of Jamie's cock straining against the cloth. "Dinner first, then we'll have dessert."

Shifting in the seat a bit more, Jamie fought like hell to keep his attention on the road. "Harder." He reached down and pressed Adrian's hand against him. "Fuck," he hissed. "Yeah. Food. Then fucking. Lots of fucking."

The press of his hand rubbed slowly against Jamie as he watched him intently. He enjoyed the effect he had on the cowboy, and it took little to make them both hard. Slowly, he withdrew his hand. "That's exactly what's on the menu."

Jamie let out a breath of relief as he turned off the truck in front of Adrian's apartment building. But instead of getting out, he moved the bags onto the top of the dashboard and reached out for Adrian. Taking a fistful of Adrian's shirt in hand, Jamie tugged him close, practically shoving his tongue down Adrian's throat.

Not expecting the action, Adrian's hand stilled on the door handle. Leaning in towards Jamie, his mouth tightened around his tongue in mimic of fucking. Before Jamie could pull away, Adrian's tongue slid into his mouth, lengthening the kiss.

After fumbling with their seatbelts, Jamie finally got them undone with his other hand. Then he slid across the cab and straddled Adrian's thighs, grinding down hard as he deepened the kiss.

"Need you," he whispered. "Oh, fuck, I need you."

Adrian actually hadn't meant things to get out of hand, but feeling Jamie rocking against him, all he could think about was the same need. Drawing a ragged breath, he lifted his hands to Jamie's face. "We need to get into the apartment, cowboy. Before I fuck you in the truck."

"Come on," Jamie panted as he crawled off Adrian. "Inside. Now. Need to take the fucking edge off." Grabbing the bags of food, he got out of the truck, body almost humming with sheer need.

Adrian was right behind Jamie. The minute they were inside the apartment, he took the bags of food and set them on the table by the door. When his hands were free, he unsnapped Jamie's pants and tugged them down. His other hand unfastened his own pants. Being completely intent on his purpose, Adrian barely stayed steady.

Hands on Adrian's shoulders, Jamie leaned back against the door, pushing his tongue into Adrian's mouth. Feeling hard flesh slide along his own, he gasped into the kiss, pushing frantically against Adrian, sliding their cocks together.

Leaning against Jamie, Adrian's hand slid between them, fingers curling around both of their cocks. His hand pulled slowly over both of them in leisurely tugs that quickened with the rise of his own need to come. Placing the other hand flat against the wall near Jamie's hand, Adrian wanted the support. His knees were already weakening with the delicious friction of their cocks rubbing together.

"Oh. Fuck," Jamie gasped, tearing away from the kiss to suck in a sharp breath. "Don't stop. Fuck, Adrian, don't stop." He curled his fingers tighter on Adrian's shoulders, thrusting and bucking against Adrian. Just like that, lightning shot up his spine and his head slammed back against the door. He shuddered hard as he came, heat spilling over Adrian's fist.

"Jamie." Adrian called to him in a quickly exhaled breath. The sound of his lover, and slippery feel of liquid coating his hand, sent Adrian over the edge. A deep shudder coursed through his body with his release. Bowing his head, his body gave one last jerk before he started to come down.

"Whoa." Jamie let his head fall forward onto Adrian's shoulder. "Needed that. Bad. Food now.

More sex after."

"When I catch my breath, we will." Adrian pulled away from Jamie to toe off his shoes and get rid of his pants. In the kitchen, he washed off his hand before getting dishes and utensils out of the cupboard.

Stepping out of his jeans, Jamie went into the kitchen, sliding his hand along the small of Adrian's back as he reached for the plates on the counter. The moment felt perfect, almost enough that he opened his mouth, ready to say three little words. Stopping himself before he could do something stupid, he just kissed Adrian's shoulder.

"Dinnertime, gorgeous."

"Tomorrow is going to be my treat." Turning his head to look at Jamie, Adrian grinned at him. " How 'bout McDonald's?"

Quickly tugging off his shirt, Adrian tossed it back towards the living room where his pants and shoes were.

"Mm," Jamie hummed softly, brushing his lips over Adrian's bare shoulder. "McDonald's is good. Their French fries are the best." He licked slowly along the curve of Adrian's neck before stepping away to set out the plates on the table. He wanted to talk, wanted to tell Adrian how he felt; but he just couldn't. Maybe he was chicken, or maybe it was because he just didn't see Adrian feeling the same.

Chuckling, Adrian headed towards the table. "Tomorrow I'll get you McDonald's and then we'll stop at Wendy's for me."

"Sounds good." Jamie got the bags of take-out and started dishing out their dinner. Settling in, he moaned softly as he took a bite of the sweet and sour chicken.

Once he had a generous helping of everything, Adrian dug into the food. "Mmm. One of my favorite restaurants. Usually I eat there on Mondays."

Both of them devoted the next several minutes to replenishing their energy. When Jamie reached for the last piece of beef, Adrian speared it quickly with his fork. Grinning, he held it up triumphantly, waving it in front of Jamie's face. Deliberately Adrian moaned in exaggerated appreciation as he ate it.

Laughing, Jamie snagged a fortune cookie.

"Oh, yeah." Once he was full, Jamie sat back, grateful he'd already lost the jeans. "Damn, that was good."

Adrian gave him a lazy smile as his focus returned to the cowboy. The view of Jamie naked beneath the table, yet still in his shirt, had an enticing effect on him. "I'm gonna be in the mood for dessert fairly soon."

Licking his lips, Jamie pulled his shirt over his head, tossing it to the side. "You gonna give this cowboy a ride? Need something hard, deep inside me…" As his words trailed off, Jamie leaned back and put his feet on the edge of the table, spreading his legs open for Adrian. He began stroking his cock idly, the other hand moving up to tweak one of his nipples.

As Jamie leaned back, it did funny things inside Adrian. His gaze dropped to watch the slow stroke of the cowboy's hand. The stirring in his groin wasn't that much of a surprise to him. Jamie seemed to affect him with very little effort. The sight of his lover naked and playing with himself had Adrian off the chair.

"What do you want, pretty boy?" Jamie bit his lip and groaned softly, sliding lower in the chair until his ass was hanging off the edge. He sucked a finger into his mouth, then lowered it to circle over his hole, not quite pushing it inside.

Leaning over, the light brush of his fingers ran over the length of Jamie's cock as he watched him. "I wanna ride a hot cowboy. Ride him fast and hard until he screams my name."

The tip of his finger traced slowly over the head of Jamie's cock, gathering the drops Adrian's eyes never left his as he licked them off his finger.

Jamie's eyes clouded over as he pushed the finger inside himself. "Yeah. Oh, fuck, yes. Ride me hard, Adrian." His body jerked under Adrian's touch. "Hard and fucking deep."

A soft groan of sound escaped Adrian as his eyes roamed over Jamie's writhing body. He ended up brushing Jamie's hand away, his already wet finger replacing Jamie's. Rubbing slowly against his prostate, he knelt to the side, taking Jamie's cock in his mouth. The slow slid of his mouth engulfed him in a leisurely motion as if he had all the time in the world, and he did.

"Oh. Fuck." Jamie slid both hands through Adrian's hair, caught between thrusting up into his mouth and grinding down on Adrian's finger. "More. Need more, Adrian. Fill me."

Slowly he inserted another finger as his mouth worked slowly over Jamie. It would take a bit of time, and Jamie was definitely hanging on the edge.

Adding another finger, Adrian continued the slow, torturous stroking over the sensitive gland.

"Adrian." Jamie's head fell back against the chair and he started riding Adrian's fingers, driving them deeper. "More," he whispered hoarsely. God, he was shaking, needing so bad. "Don't stop. Don't stop."

Never increasing the tempo, he let Jamie ride the needful urges. Listening to his cries, he savored the pleading edge to the cowboy's voice. His tongue swirled around Jamie's cock with the glide of his mouth as his fingers played inside him. When Adrian couldn't take anymore, he released Jamie from his mouth, and his fingers withdrew from him.

"In the bed, Jamie. Now." His voice was rough, tinged with his own rising need to fuck Jamie. It'd already become near uncontrollable.

"Yeah." Standing on shaky legs, Jamie grabbed Adrian's hand and pulled him down the hall. In the bedroom, he collapsed onto the bed, tugging Adrian down on top of him. "Fuck. Me."

As Adrian fell on top of him, he fumbled, opening the drawer to get the rubber and lube out. With an impatient tear of his teeth, he opened the rubber. Hastily rolling it onto his cock, he used the lube to slick over the rubber. Having already spent enough time preparing, his hand guided his cock downward and a hard shove of his hips pushed him inside Jamie.

Jamie gasped and rocked his hips up, meeting the thrust. His fingers tangled in Adrian's hair and he pulled him down, licking at Adrian's lips before pushing his tongue between them. Legs spread wide, he wrapped them around Adrian's waist, holding him close and rocking beneath him.

"Yes," he murmured. "Oh, fuck, yes. Feels so fucking good, Adrian. So goddamned good."

The tight heat surrounding Adrian sharply increased the tension of his body. Sliding his hand down to Jamie's hip, his fingers took tight hold of him. No holds barred, he rode his cowboy with a ruthless, jarring force. His breath escaped him in gasps of sound. Relentless, he pounded into Jamie's ass, feeling the tightness of muscle surrounding his cock.

"Adrian!" Arching his back, Jamie dragged his nails down Adrian's spine, head tipping back as he took everything Adrian gave him. Every hard thrust drove Adrian's cock across his gland, sending lightning shooting straight up Jamie's spine. "Fuck, fuck, fuck... Oh, God..."

Every cry from Jamie sounded like the sweetest music. Releasing his hip, Adrian's hand curled to Jamie's cock. Sensations doubled with each thrust of his hips and stroke of his hand. Even near lost in the rising lust, he wanted his lover to tumble completely into everything he could give him. Brushing a soft kiss to his lips, Adrian whispered, "Let me feel you lose it."

Raising his head, he heatedly stared down at Jamie. Deliberately, he shifted the cowboy's leg higher to deepen the force of his movements. As much as he wanted his own pleasure, he wanted to fulfill Jamie's even more. Adrian's fingers curled quickly around his cock, mimicking the forceful thrusts of his hips.

"Adrian..." Jamie's eyes widened seconds before

his body went taut. Digging his fingers into Adrian's back, he shouted Adrian's name as he shot, hips bucking hard and fast.

Adrian rode through Jamie's orgasm, his eyes refusing to leave him. As he watched his lover drown in the intensity, he lost it as well. His own release rushed through him, a shuddering spasm of exquisite waves of pleasure. He could barely form the name. "Jamie."

Jamie tugged Adrian down for a kiss, clinging to him as they both came down slowly. He licked and kissed Adrian's lips, thinking the words he knew he couldn't say.

Collapsing on him, Adrian struggled for breath. It took him a moment to return the soft affection. With a groan, he withdrew and rolled off to his side. After peeling off the rubber, he tossed it in the small trash can next to the bed. "I think I'm gonna need a breather before we do anything else."

"I agree." Jamie chuckled and rolled over, curling around Adrian. "This feels good, too."

Sliding his arm around him, Adrian turned his head slightly, brushing a soft kiss to his hair. "Not going to argue with you on that. For once my apartment is peaceful."

"It's a start. Lord Almighty, you have some interesting friends." Jamie shifted until he could see Adrian's face. Lifting a hand, he stroked his fingers over Adrian's cheek. "God, you're something else."

"So are you, cowboy. You wear me out." Chuckling, he caught Jamie's hand and brought it to his lips. His tongue darted out, teasingly licking at the length of one of his fingers. "They broke the mold when they made me. Or so my ole da says." Keeping a hold of Jamie's hand, he drew it to his chest.

Moving his hand slightly to rest it over Adrian's heart, Jamie looked into his eyes. After a few minutes of silence, he said quietly, "Yeah, they did."

"Gerald wanted to know if you were going to drop by next Friday. He said he'd appreciate the company if you wanted to. Lucy wants me to take her to Aunt Em's house so I won't be able to go over to Gerald's."

Jamie thought for a moment. "It really depends on how much work I can get done between now and then. One of DeSalvo's pieces is nearing completion, and I still have orders coming in. I'll do my best, though."

Nodding to him, Adrian relaxed beside him. "He's looking for a beer buddy. Remind me to give you his number before I fall asleep. Call him if you can head over there."

"Will do," Jamie whispered. He kissed Adrian's hair and held him close, ignoring the ache somewhere deep inside.

Turning towards him, Adrian nuzzled in against Jamie's chest. The warmth of his breath played over Jamie's skin as he sighed quietly. "Are we going to continue to laze in bed or get up for a bit?"

"How about a movie?"

"I'll probably fall asleep in the middle of it." Laughing, he moved to the edge of the bed and stood up. "Want any snacks or you still good from dinner?"

Adrian headed down the hall to the kitchen. Opening the fridge, he got out the pitcher of juice to pour himself a glass.

"I'm still good." Jamie grabbed the blanket from the bed and carried it into the living room. "What do you suggest?" he asked as he dropped the blanket on the couch and started looking through Adrian's DVDs.

"I'm a fan of Abbot and Costello, if you couldn't tell. Put in one of them." Putting the juice back in the fridge, he picked up his glass and headed into the living room.

Chuckling, Jamie pulled out *Abbot and Costello Meet the Mummy*. "I never would've guessed." After putting it into the player, he grabbed the remote and joined Adrian on the couch, pulling the blanket up around them. Then he slid an arm around Adrian and held him close as the movie started.

Settling in, Adrian laughed. "Marx Brothers, The Three Stooges, you name an old comedy, and I love it."

These nights together were getting to be a serious habit with them. Jamie could feel him relaxing against him so Adrian didn't seem to mind at all either.

Jamie's mind was anywhere but on the movie. He was getting too attached, too deep in this than he figured Adrian would be comfortable hearing. It hurt like hell to admit it when he just didn't see Adrian feeling the same, but Jamie knew his own feelings like he knew the sun would rise. He was thoroughly, head over heels in love.

After finishing his juice, Adrian set the empty glass on the end. As he stretched out on the length of the couch, he pulled Jamie with him, spooning his back against the cowboy. The flickering light of the

TV set left the rest of the room in the shadows. "Maybe after this we'll watch *Hold That Ghost*."

When Jamie shifted against him, he scooted deeper into the couch before resettling. In the comfortable silence he watched the movie with Jamie. It wasn't until half way through the second movie that Adrian started to drift off. With a start, he woke up with a yawn. "I think we need to get to bed, Jamie. I'm ready to fall asleep."

Once they'd settled in the bed, Adrian fell deeply asleep shortly after his head hit the pillow. Jamie waited until Adrian had been sleeping for a half an hour before getting up. After tucking the blanket around Adrian, he got dressed as quietly as possible. Then he sat down at the dining room table and started to write. He hated this, absolutely hated it. But he honestly had no idea what else to do.

A few minutes later, he felt sick, the feeling worsening as he read over the note for the fifth time. He went into the bedroom and looked at Adrian, hoping he was doing the right thing. Adrian was young and had too much on him as it was; the last thing Jamie figured the kid needed was a middle-aged cowboy falling in love with him. And unrequited love just—hurt. Best to walk away now.

He put the note on the bedside table, along with a single white rose for faith—faith that he was doing the right thing by letting Adrian go. He leaned over and kissed those sweet lips one last time, then left Adrian's apartment, resisting the urge to look back.

PART SIX

Adrian,

When I first met you, I was only looking for some fun. I tried to keep things that way; I tried not to care too much. Guess I failed miserably there.

I can't do this anymore, Adrian. I've grown to care about you more than I think I should. I'm sorry.

Sincerely,
Jamie

After reading the note for the tenth time, Adrian crushed the paper in his fist. What the fuck had happened? He'd believed both of them were happy. Smoothing out the wrinkled paper with his hand, he realized he'd obviously been wrong. Jamie had dropped him. The blow hit him out of nowhere, and left him reeling.

Reaching for the phone, Adrian dialed Jamie's work number. When there was no answer, he hung up. Indecisively he stared at the phone before he dialed Jamie's home number. Jamie's answering machine picked up the call and he said, "Jamie, it's Adrian. Call me."

Somehow Adrian managed to get dressed and get out of the apartment to head to DeSalvo's estate. By late afternoon, he still hadn't gotten a call from Jamie. Using his cell phone, he called Jamie's house again. This time the message he left sounded bewildered and angry. "Call me, dammit."

When Eric entered the office, Adrian snapped his cell phone shut and shoved it into his pocket. It proved to be several long hours before he returned to the peace and quiet of his apartment.

Over the next two nights, Adrian kept the same vigil. Settled at the edge of his bed, he stared at the phone. The crumpled ball of paper, and dying white rose, laid next to it. The glowing red numbers on his clock told him it was three AM. He hadn't slept the night before, and still couldn't get to sleep. He remained sitting tensely, his gaze drifting between the phone and wadded paper. Jamie wasn't going to call him back. Adrian realized the message with clarity of thought that burned through him with its own pain. Jamie wasn't coming back at all. God, how that hurt. He had to resist the urge to grab the phone and throw it against the wall.

Tightness closed in his throat, forcing him to swallow against the rise of sudden tears and emotion. His lover had indeed deserted him, and he was no closer to the truth of why. So what if Jamie had feelings for him? He didn't give a flying fuck, he just wanted the cowboy back. And he wasn't even given the chance to say it.

The tears finally spilled free as he curled up on the bed, staring blindly at the clock. No matter how hard he fought, Adrian couldn't stop or control the pain flooding him. His blurry gaze fixated on the phone, and it wasn't until his alarm clock sounded that he realized sleep had eluded him again.

Wearily, he dragged himself out of bed to face his day. Every hour that went by killed Adrian's last fading hope Jamie would call him. In a daze, Adrian functioned but barely. His surroundings, and even time, lost meaning to the growing pain swallowing him whole.

* * * *

Lighting up his third cigarette, Jamie kicked at a stone lodged in the grass. He'd driven out here, even managed to get the damned truck turned off this time; but fuck if he could make himself walk the short distance to Adrian's front door. It'd taken him a week to get this far.

He took a long, slow drag from the cigarette and stared at the sun as it started to dip behind the trees separating the parking lot from the road. It'd been so long since he'd fallen in love that he'd forgotten how much it could turn your stomach inside out. He'd spent half the morning between the bed and the bathroom, fighting a losing battle.

Oh, who the fuck was he kidding? He'd lost that battle a while ago. Now he wondered if he had the gumption to walk up there and just lay it out all for Adrian to see. He took another puff off the Marlboro and blew it out towards the sunset.

"Don't you dare be gone long!" Lucy's screech followed Adrian as he opened the door and stepped outside. Looking over his shoulder, he yelled back, "I said I'm only running to the store."

Not looking where he was going, Adrian barreled right into Jamie.

"Oh, man, sorry..." he trailed off as he saw Jamie. Pain flickered in his eyes before it could be hidden. "Oh, God, Jamie."

Jamie opened his mouth, then snapped it shut.

Fuck. He wasn't expecting things to happen quite like this. He was supposed to knock on the door. Adrian was supposed to look at him like he was a ghost. Jamie had prepared himself for all that.

What he hadn't prepared himself for was the pain in Adrian's eyes. Damn.

"I…" Biting his lip, he looked to the side for a moment, not quite able to look into Adrian's eyes. If he did, he'd lose it right here in the fucking parking lot. "I wondered if we could talk."

For a moment, Adrian didn't say anything at all. He just stared at Jamie, reeling in shock. "Yeah." It was a moment later before he thought to add. "Come on upstairs."

Turning away from him, Adrian headed back into the apartment building.

Swallowing the lump in his throat and crushing his cigarette in the ashtray urn, Jamie followed behind Adrian. He made a point to look anywhere but directly at him; he still wasn't sure how Adrian would react to what he wanted to say. What he had to say.

Once inside the apartment, Jamie took his hat off and fingered the brim nervously as Adrian closed the door. He gave Lucy a slight nod, but simply couldn't find a smile.

To say the living room was packed would be an understatement. There wasn't a bare spot in the room. Most of Adrian's neighbors were either lounging in his chairs, on the floor or plastered to the wall. All of them were intently focused on one lone man. Dressed in holey, faded jeans, and a black sweater, the guy looked like an overly skinny youth nobody would be impressed with. Lucy stood beside him, all smiles, as he knelt in front of a small child, slowly passing his hands over him.

"Nostradamus, please take care of my Jason. I don't know where else to turn." A woman, obviously the boy's mother, pleaded with the young man.

Ignoring the crowd, Adrian pulled Jamie back towards the bedroom. It was the only room in the apartment that was empty.

"It's healing day," Adrian muttered before he shut the bedroom door, blocking out the throng in the rest of his apartment.

Jamie made a mental note to ask about the menagerie in the living room—if he had the chance. As it was, when they got to the bedroom, he didn't move away from the door. He looked down at his hat and cleared his throat. God, the noise sounded so loud.

"I'm sorry, Adrian."

Adrian stood staring at him for a long moment then finally asked, "Why, Jamie? Why did you leave me?"

Abruptly, Adrian bit back any more questions, looking confused before he turned away from Jamie.

Here it was, time to come clean. Jamie looked up, almost grateful that Adrian's back was to him, because his next words had the potential to kill him if Adrian didn't like what he had to say.

"Because I was starting to care more deeply for you than I thought you wanted." Okay, so it was a roundabout way of saying it.

"You never asked me what I wanted. You just left. You didn't give me a choice at all, and it fucking hurt." Moving away from Jamie, he went towards the window and stared out at the street.

God, he hated this. Jamie closed his eyes for a minute, then steeled himself to go up to Adrian. He wanted to reach out to him, wanted to hold him, to kiss him. Anything but this.

"I left when just seeing you became painful, Adrian." Sighing with frustration, he just spilled it out right there. "I left because I love you so much, it fucking hurts."

Slowly turning to face him, Adrian simply stared at him again. "Couldn't you have told me that before?"

Without thought, he raised his hand to Jamie's lip, fingertips slowly brushing to them. "It hurt when I woke up and found you gone. I didn't think you were ever coming back to me."

Jamie closed his eyes. God, he wanted to pull Adrian into his arms and just start over. Just forget they were here, now, feeling miles apart.

"I didn't know how to," he said quietly. He kissed Adrian's fingers softly. "I was so afraid of losing you. I still am, but I'm here. I'm spilling everything out now, hoping like hell that you won't turn me away."

Lowering his hand, he sighed quietly. A struggle was evident in his features as if he were at war with himself. "Jamie, I don't know how I feel about you. The only thing I know is I need you to be with me."

"I'm not leaving again. Just promise me that you'll tell me if this isn't what you ultimately want. I'm too old to go through the motions, Adrian. I love you. Nothing will change that."

"I'm not sure it's fair to keep you around when I don't know myself."

Jamie reached out and slipped his hand around the back of Adrian's neck to pull him close. "You're worth waiting for," he whispered. "I can't let you go."

As Jamie pulled him close, Adrian bowed his head. Closing his eyes, he burrowed in against the cowboy's chest. "I understand why you left me. Everything is risk, more for you than me. I only hope neither of us regrets it. I missed you. I missed waking up to you smiling at me."

Slipping his fingers under Adrian's chin, Jamie tilted Adrian's head back to see his eyes. "I just missed waking up to you. You're a hard habit to break, love." He leaned in and kissed Adrian softly, not moving it any further than a kiss of peace. He'd let Adrian decide if things would go beyond that.

His arms slid around Jamie's waist, keeping him close. Returning the light kiss, he began to relax against the cowboy. "We've got a bit to make up for. Hell, we have a lot to make up for."

The push of his body urged Jamie towards the bed behind them as he added, "You're not going anywhere until I'm thoroughly satisfied we've both made up for it."

Jamie tossed his hat onto the dresser. "I'm not leaving until you kick me out." Gripping Adrian's chin, Jamie kissed him again. With the first taste, he moaned into the kiss. He backed onto the bed and pulled Adrian down on top of him, never breaking the possessive tenor of his kiss.

Tumbling down to the bed, Adrian's hand ran along Jamie's side as his body pinned Jamie to the bed. It took very little to bring out the hungering need between them. His lips tightened on Jamie's, tasting his mouth and the small sound.

Breaking the kiss for only a moment, Jamie tugged Adrian's shirt off, then dove back in, devouring Adrian's mouth as the kiss grew from exploring to outright hunger. He rolled them over and ground his hips against Adrian as he worked his way down Adrian's throat, nipping and licking. When he had Adrian's pants undone, he slid down and licked Adrian's cock from the base to the tip.

Adrian quickly struggled out of his pants. Once they'd been tossed over the side of the bed, he stretched out beneath Jamie. His breath exhaled in a sharp gasp as Jamie's tongue circled around the head of his cock. "Ah fuck, yeah, Jamie. I need your mouth."

A small jerk of his hips responded to the stimulation as his hand moved to Jamie's hair.

Keeping his eyes locked onto Adrian's, Jamie surrounded the tip with his lips and slid down, letting his throat relax as he took all of Adrian in. Oh, fuck, yes. He'd missed this, missed the bittersweet taste, the fullness as Adrian filled his mouth. Pulling back up, he let his teeth gently graze the underside. When he reached the tip, he probed the slit with his tongue, then dropped back down, starting a sucking motion over half of Adrian's cock.

Adrian's body squirmed with the feel of Jamie's mouth. Every sensation spread outward from his groin, causing him to moan. His fingers flexed tightly in his hair as his hips bucked slightly, wanting to feel the hot sheath of his whole mouth again. He held

Jamie's gaze until the welter of feelings strengthened, and he closed his eyes with another soft groan. His head pressed into the pillow as a slow tremor raced through him.

Jamie slipped a finger into his mouth alongside Adrian's cock, then slid it down. As he pushed it gently inside Adrian, he deep-throated him again, tongue sliding along the length as he curled his finger forward. Pressing and stroking Adrian's gland, he pulled back up, keeping a firm but gentle pressure along Adrian's shaft with his teeth and tongue.

"Fuck, Jamie, fuck." Adrian damn near lost it as Jamie's finger and mouth sent jolts of pure pleasure straight through him. His muscles tightened with the increasing tension, and his legs started to shake. A rising desperate need made him thrust repeatedly into Jamie's willing mouth.

One hard jerk of his hips buried him deeply in Jamie's mouth as his body shook with his orgasm. The building waves crashed over him before another hard pulse washed over him. As he came in Jamie's mouth, he cried out. The sounds only fading as his body relaxed slowly.

Jamie licked Adrian clean, slid up for a kiss, rocking and grinding against Adrian's thigh. "Need you. God, I need you so much, Adrian."

Both of them needed the affirming closeness. His hands reached for Jamie, drawing his head down for a hungry kiss. Adrian's legs wrapped to Jamie's, and he positioned his body to give Jamie what he wanted.

Jamie was reluctant to end the kiss, but there

were necessary precautions to tend to. Licking at Adrian's lips, he said, "Don't move."

He got up on his knees and reached into the bedside table drawer, knowing the rubbers and lube would be there. As he sheathed his cock in latex, he slicked up two fingers, then leaned back down, sliding them deep into Adrian's body.

"Missed this," he whispered, working his fingers in and out of Adrian. "Missed you, babe."

He'd wanted to say something to Jamie, but Adrian lost track of the thought as he felt the fingers inside him. Drawing a deep breath, the words came out in a shaky voice. "It's just you now."

Running his hands along Jamie's arms, Adrian stared up at him. He'd learned the hard way he did have his own emotions about his lover, and he refused to live without him.

"Good," Jamie whispered as he pulled his fingers out slowly, "because I don't share well." With that, he pressed in, cock sliding deep into Adrian's body. "Oh, God." He rested his forehead to Adrian's, struggling already to catch his breath.

Adrian's fingers clenched tightly as Jamie's cock stretched his ass. "Wanted to tell you no rubber."

His legs tightened around the cowboy, holding him in place. Wanting to keep the sensation that filled him, inner muscles tightened, increasing the feeling. He really didn't think they needed the protection anymore.

"That can be fixed." Without missing a beat, Jamie pulled out completely, long enough to snap off the condom, then slid back in, gasping as flesh met heated flesh. "Adrian…"

He hadn't expected Jamie to do that. A gasp escaped him as well. There was something far more intimate about leaving out the rubber. "Fuck, Jamie. Just fuck me."

"No." Buried to the hilt inside Adrian, Jamie stilled, content to kiss him deeply for a moment before continuing. "This isn't about fucking," he murmured across Adrian's cheek and down to his ear. "This is about making love." Only then did he start to move; long, slow strokes deep inside Adrian over and over again.

Understanding both the words and the feelings behind them, Adrian pressed several soft kisses to Jamie's lips. His hips matched the rhythm set by Jamie with slow, grinding rocks. Adrian felt his own emotional connection with his cowboy. Studying Jamie's face, he stayed focused on the intensity of his expression. "I don't think I need to see anyone but you."

Jamie could only keep the slow rhythm for so long before need overrode everything else. The speed and strength of his movements increased, driving him in and out Adrian's body as he took Adrian's mouth in a deep, hungry kiss. Slipping a hand between them, he curled it around Adrian's newly-awakened cock and started stroking, thumb sliding over the tip with every upstroke.

For the first time in his life, Adrian focused himself more on everything underneath the actions. Fucking was fucking, but this was something entirely different. The feel of Jamie's cock inside him strengthened the need, and his hand stroked the internal fire even more. Gasping, he met the quickening drive into his body. Adrian's lips clung to Jamie's beneath the kiss as his fingers tangled tightly in his hair.

"Need you, want you...love you," Jamie said, accentuating each statement with a kiss. His movements tightening, Jamie drove harder and deeper, his strokes over Adrian's cock determined and sure.

"Need you more than anything." He opened himself in the moment of honesty as the pleasure caused him to writhe beneath Jamie. Jamie pushed him over the edge into a deep shuddering orgasm that swept his body. Before it could even fade, his hips jerked hard against Jamie's hand with the next pulses hitting him. As he came again, the liquid coated their bodies.

"Adrian. Love..." Jamie gasped and thrust hard, hips jerking against Adrian's ass as he came. For several minutes after, he simply couldn't move. Reluctant to pull out of the tight heat of Adrian's body, he settled over him, kissing Adrian softly but thoroughly. "I love you. So much."

Moments later when Adrian had finally calmed his breathing, he smiled up at Jamie. Savoring the weight of Jamie's body, he stretched slightly beneath him. "I know I care a great deal about you. I don't want to live without you."

"You won't have to, love," Jamie murmured. "I won't ever let you go again."

"You can handle that?" Giving him a searching look, Adrian reached up, touching his face. The only thing troubling Adrian was whether or not Jamie could really deal with Adrian not loving him.

Eventually he might, but in the meantime he was afraid it might cause Jamie pain.

Easing out of Adrian, Jamie settled beside him, rolling onto his side to look into Adrian's eyes. "I left because it hurt to love and not be loved back," he said finally, "but I came back because I simply can't live without you, Adrian." Reaching up, he touched Adrian's lips softly with his fingertips. "I know that you care a lot for me, and for me, that's a start. You're worth waiting for."

Relaxing with the words, Adrian let go of the tension he hadn't even realized had crept up on him. Pressing a kiss to the touch of his finger, he spoke quietly, "I just needed to know. I don't think I can deal with you taking off on me again. It hurt too much."

"I know, and I'm so sorry. I promise you: never again, Adrian."

Nodding to him in acceptance of the promise, Adrian smiled again. "Next time we'll just talk about our problems."

"Agreed." Leaning over, Jamie kissed him again, finally at peace with himself, and with them.

About the Authors

Mychael Black never set out to write erotic romance (or romance or erotica, for that matter). When Mychael first started writing (way back when), it was to be a fantasy author — someone along the lines of Tolkien or Mercedes Lackey. Mychael even thought about breaking into horror. Then, somewhere down the line, Mychael got hooked on gay porn.

The rest is history.

Born in Alabama in 1976, Mychael is known by many names. At this point, most people in the e-publishing world (readers and authors) know Mychael as Kay Derwydd.

The name Mychael Black came about when Mychael started working with Shayne Carmichael. (See Shayne's bio for the progression of that whole thing.) To date, Mychael has written countless works with Shayne, plus several single-authored works as Mychael Black.

When not writing, Mychael can usually be found researching anything medieval — arms, armor, history, religion; anything Welsh — culture, language, history; languages—namely Welsh, Hebrew, German; and only God knows what else.

Aside from research, writing, and editing, Mychael spends most of the time chasing down two young children and fighting off the plot bunnies left and right.

More information can be found at the following places:

http://www.geocities.com/mychaelblack
http://mychael-black2.livejournal.com

Who is **Shayne Carmichael**? His real name is Shayne Lee Smith. He was born in Itazuke, Japan to American parents. (ie - Dad was in the Air Force). From the age of three to eight, he lived in Taiwan. He's traveled a lot, and only discovered even more he wants to learn about the world.

When not writing, Shayne is a self taught PHP and MySql dynamo. Or at least one would think from the number of scripts he's been begged to write for free. With any spare time left to him, Shayne runs ERWI (Erotic Romance Writers International), aggravates his co-author, Mychael, to no end, often drowns under Mychael's plot bunnies, and holds a forty hour a week job.

Currently Shayne is working on a six book series, The Legends of the Romanorum. Blood Ties, Blood Magic and Blood Sins are being written by Shayne.

The Prince's Angel, And the Two Shall Become One, and Forever May Not Be Long Enough are being written by Shayne and Mychael. Included in the writing list are a few other books, Magic and the Pagan, Night Song, and numerous novellas and shorts.

Shayne writes under the pen names of Sable St Germain and Shayne Carmichael. Sable was an RP character he used to play. Shayne Carmichael is a combination of his first name and Cian's (Angel/sorcerer in The Prince's Angel) last name. The character Shayne writes for in The Prince's Angel is Mael Black. That would explain why Mychael's last name is Black, and the character Mychael writes for is Cian.

Shayne's first official publishing contact is with Phaze for the Power of Two. A vampire D/s, BDSM story written with Mychael Black. The status of Phaze author has been one of their goals. Having achieved that, their next goal is to take over the world.

Over the last nine years, Shayne has rped (roleplayed) and written both male and female characters. Gay, lesbian and het (vanilla and non vanilla). You could say he runs the gamut.

He's never believed whatever gender he happens to possess dictates what he can and can't write. And he pretty much ignores anybody who thinks that way. Especially since he's never been a vampire, were tiger, ghost or guide, but he writes about them anyway.

Hell, he could be a woman pretending to be a man, or a man pretending to be a woman. He might be a 21 year old sex crazed female or a 60 year old dirty old man. It's the world wide anonymous web, remember? In the anonymous vacuum of web space, nobody can hear you scream. They can't tell your age or sex either.

In the publication of most of his books and for advertising, his persona is male. In the comic strip The Beleaguered Lives of Mychael and Shayne, his persona is female. Why? He likes confusing the readers. Then again, maybe he's a bit of both.

Whether he's a man writing gay, lesbian and kinky het or a woman writing gay, lesbian and kinky het, doesn't matter. If he can draw you into a story with his words, he's done his job.

Who is Shayne Carmichael? Does it really matter?

Shayne shares a website with Mychael Black, his partner in crime at http://www.theprinceangel.com. Excerpts for other works and several freebie stories are available on the site. To contact Shayne, email shayne@theprincesangel.com.

Printed in the United States
141959LV00001B/75/P

9 781606 590287